D0040776

DEAD
in
the
WATER

To Roger,

Dive into a great read!

DEAD in the WATER

Margaret Hoffman

Margaret Hoffman

Coastal Plains Publishing Company

Raleigh, North Carolina

Published in Raleigh, North Carolina
by Coastal Plains Publishing Company

Coastal Plains Publishing Company
3116-27 Dockside Circle
Raleigh, NC 27613
(919) 788-9539

ISBN: #0-9607300-2-8

First Edition

Library of Congress Control Number: 2003100138

To Bruce Smith

A fictional work inspired from a true incident and the following sources:

"Local diver describes dramatic rescue.
Weekend expedition clouded by ordeal."
— *Santa Barbara News-Press*

"Last-minute rescue saves scuba divers after they
defy death for 14 hours in undersea air chamber."
— *The Ventura Star*

"Sheriff team saves pair trapped in underwater cave."
— *Ventura County Star Free Press*

"Rescued from Submerged Cave.
2 Divers Trapped 14 Hours."
— *Los Angeles Times*

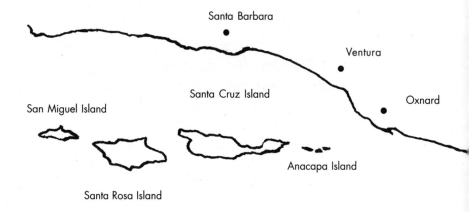

Santa Barbara

Ventura

Oxnard

Santa Cruz Island

San Miguel Island

Santa Rosa Island

Anacapa Island

Santa Barbara Island

San Nicholas Island

California's Channel Islands

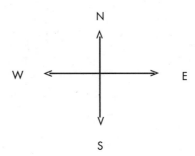

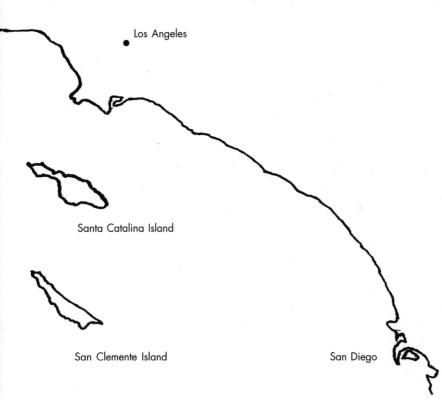

Los Angeles

Santa Catalina Island

San Clemente Island

San Diego

PREFACE

Sometimes a writer hears a true story that is so fascinating that he or she instinctively knows it is material for a novel.

Such was the case one snowy December day in the mid-90s when Bruce Smith of Santa Barbara, California, then stationed in Washington, DC at the Bethesda Naval Hospital, told me of his near-death experience at Santa Cruz Island. We were watching a film, *Apollo 13*. I believe it was the suffocating feeling of lack of air that sparked his memory; or perhaps, it was just homesickness for California at Christmas, but he told me about an incident that was so haunting, I had to put pen to paper.

The incident occurred on December 3, 1979 when he left the Santa Barbara Marina for a weekend scuba diving trip with his friends to Santa Cruz Island. He became trapped in an undersea cave for fourteen hours.

Bruce's rescue was the first time in the history of the Ventura County Search and Rescue dive team that a victim had been brought up alive from a cave on the Channel Islands. Because of this miraculous rescue, members of the team changed the name of the dive unit from Search and

Recovery to Search and Rescue.

The Channel Islands are situated just off California's coast. Five of these islands (Anacapa, Santa Cruz, Santa Rosa, San Miguel and Santa Barbara) and their surrounding one nautical mile of kelp forests and ocean comprise the Channel Islands National Park. Scattered throughout are caves, many of which are on intersecting fault lines forming complex mazes that lead in all directions — a labyrinth of unexplored passageways. Southern California newspapers often report divers who discover these caves, get lost in the mazes and die.

On Santa Cruz, there are 120 known caves. Twenty-six are over 300 feet long and forty-six are over 200 feet long. Some of these caves can be entered above water and some are submerged.

It was in one of these caves beneath Santa Cruz, the largest of the eight islands, that Bruce found himself on that fateful afternoon. He entered Seals Cove Submerged Cave. It is entirely submerged, and requires scuba gear, bright lights and specialized dive training. It is unmapped and the length unknown, although 400 feet of dive line have been laid without reaching an end. It is considered to be the most dangerous cave on Santa Cruz Island.

Only by a series of startling coincidences, seemingly more fiction than fact, was Bruce able to survive that day in this cave. Many divers, finding themselves in the same situation, have not been so lucky.

Although inspired from Bruce's life-and-death drama, this is not a true story. It is a contemporary suspense novel containing some elements of the original event. It is fictional, as are the characters, and any resemblance to real people is entirely coincidental.

ACKNOWLEDGEMENTS

Bruce's real story gave me the background for my novel and for that I am extremely grateful. The story was published in the following newspapers shortly after the event took place: Gerry Levin, "Last-minute rescue saves scuba divers after they defy death for 14 hours in undersea air chamber," *The Star,* January 8, 1980; Bill Milton, "Local diver describes dramatic rescue," *Santa Barbara News-Press*, December 4, 1979; Jim McLain, "Sheriff team saves pair trapped in underwater cave," *Ventura County Star Free Press*, December 3, 1979; and John Kendall, "Rescued from Submerged Cave, 2 Divers Trapped 14 Hours," *Los Angeles Times*, December 4, 1979.

In addition, I would also like to thank the following people for their help: my father, Julian Hoffman of Danville, Virginia for his artwork on the front and back jacket and his map of the Channel Islands; Mike Everett of Raleigh, North Carolina for editing the book; Leona Reed of California Tourism; Malei Weir and the Ventura Visitors and Convention Bureau; the Channel Islands National Park staff, with a special thanks to Tom Dore for his knowledge of diving, boating and the Channel Islands; the Island Packers cruises of Ventura, California for their trip to the Channel Islands; Kevin Libera and the staff of the Ventura Holiday Inn Beach Hotel and the staff of the Marriott Ventura Beach Hotel, both of which provided beautiful accommodations in Ventura, California; Ben Wofford and Mark Parker of American Marine Publishing in North Palm Beach, Florida for their boating expertise; Coast Guard Officer Bill Kelly of Raleigh, North Carolina and Coast Guard Officer Mark Fisher of Oxnard, California; James F. Smith and Scott Anthony of Ventura Dive and Sport in Ventura, California; Rick Allen of Nautilus Productions in Fayetteville, North Carolina; Sergeant Earl Matthews of the Ventura County Sheriff's Department, who was involved in the original rescue; Paul Wilderson of the Naval Institute Press; Phil Masters of Beaufort, North Carolina; David Dickieson of Washington, D.C., who has shared his legal expertise and advice throughout the years; Marilyn Lauritzen of Greensboro, North Carolina; Rae Holland of Alexandria, Virginia; Judy Cobb, formerly of Santa Barbara, California, now living in Raleigh, North Carolina; Sandra Chasak of Raleigh, North Carolina; and lastly, those people who wish to remain anonymous, but who contributed important information.

Without the input of all of these people, this novel would not have been possible.

CHAPTER

1

"WE HAVE TO TALK."

Her words rose from the digital phone like a chilling apparition.

Mike shut off the phone. A sudden tension gripped his body. He knew what was coming. Another argument.

Now driving down Highway 101 toward his home in the foothills of the Santa Ynez Mountains, he tapped his fingers nervously on the steering wheel. As he entered Montecito, the carefully manicured lawns of Santa Barbara's elite rolled past him in a green blur.

Well, he couldn't exactly blame Cathy. He'd been out of town for well over a month. His business, Mike Gallagher's Dive and Travel, often took him on extended trips to exotic resorts. Still, what wife wouldn't get angry if her husband left her for weeks on end?

Reluctantly, he gave the engine a little more gas.

As a kid, living in a two bedroom house with an alcoholic father, he used to run away from home just to avoid an argument. Now, ironically, he was driving toward a confrontation.

Hell, she knew when she married him that he wasn't a family man.

Fact was, he always had to be on the go. If he'd wanted, when he'd come out of Vietnam, he could have taken a cushy job at the Pentagon to last him right up until retirement. But he wasn't a paper pusher.

He rubbed his chin. The closer he got to home, the worse he felt. Home these days had become a place to drop his bags, do his laundry, stay awhile and entertain guests before his next trip out.

He rounded a bend and then reached in the glove compartment to pull out the electronic device that allowed him entry into a long winding driveway. The automatic wrought iron gates swung open to a multimillion-dollar Spanish estate, situated on several acres of a lawn landscaped with eucalyptus and palm trees. As he made his way up the driveway, he had a spectacular view of the Santa Barbara Harbor and the Channel Islands.

He parked his 911 Turbo beside his wife's Mercedes.

Apprehensively, he opened the back door and walked through the large airy kitchen surrounding a built-in table where Cathy cut up her herbs and vegetables. Burnished copper pots and pans hung from the rafters.

He entered the hallway lined with ceramic vases holding tropical plants.

He looked up to see his wife standing in the hallway. Her figure was silhouetted in the light streaming through a window.

She still looked great, a tall athletic woman with high cheekbones and shoulder-length honey hair, typical of Californians who spend a lot of time in the sun and sea. She smiled, revealing a set of perfect white teeth against her tanned skin, but the smile faded and turned into a steady gaze.

"Hi, hon," he said, bracing himself for the oncoming fight. He put his car keys on the hallway table and walked into the dining room.

She followed. "Mike, there's something we need to discuss."

"What's that?" He approached the bar and poured himself a scotch. He had a feeling this was serious enough to warrant a drink.

She sat down on the barstool across from an aquarium filled with rare fish he had brought back from his many trips. "You've been in Truk for a month." She swirled around on the seat to face him. "It's too long."

"I know my being away is tough on you, Cathy." He reached over and patted her gently on the shoulder.

She shook her head. "It's not just me, Mike." There was a tone of accusation in her voice.

"Look, Cathy, we're going to get a big deal soon, I just know it."

She bit her lip. "Sales of the merchandise are off, and the dive lessons are barely enough to make payments on the boat. Thousands of dollars are going out for these trips to advertise the business and get package deals on motel rooms and flights. We still owe ScubaPro and Seaquest and Capitol. I can't keep financing a failing business."

"Just give it a little time," he protested.

She looked away from him for a moment. She shook her head. "If you weren't gone so much..."

"Cathy, don't start," he interrupted, taking another shot. "The dive business is my job. It's me. It's what I do." He swept his hand through his hair and frowned.

"Well, what you do is costing us." She paused. "I had another offer for the business last week."

He shook his head. She was starting on that again. She knew damned well he didn't want to give up the business.

She gave him a sideways glance and firmly folded her arms. "Well, I've decided we need...I need a change..." Her words trailed off into silence.

He gave her a quizzical wrinkle of the eyebrow. "What kind of change?"

She pursed her lips. "I want a separation."

His heart pounded in his chest. He was so shocked, he almost spilled his drink. They'd been having arguments for years, but never before had she mentioned a separation. "Don't you think that's a little drastic?"

She shook her head. "Not really. It's been coming for a long time."

He glared at her. "So you want a divorce."

"I'm not saying that. Just a separation."

"You want a divorce," he repeated. His fear escalated into anger. He got up from the stool and turned his back on her. Abruptly, he whirled around. "You want to call it quits after fifteen years of marriage." He glared at her.

"What kind of a marriage do we have, Mike?" she argued. "You're never at home. I spend my evenings by myself, while you're off on some Caribbean island, drinking and partying, living it up and doing God knows what."

"What's that supposed to mean?"

She gritted her teeth.

"Cathy, baby," he said with a forced gentleness. "I've been perfectly faithful to you."

She folded her arms.

He had to do something to change her mind. He couldn't let her go through with her plans. "I didn't think it would come to a divorce. I don't want to lose you."

"Mike, it's just..." she began, unfolding her arms.

He took her in his arms and kissed her gently on her lips. She trembled slightly. He could feel her pent-up anger dissipating.

"I do miss you, Mike," she admitted.

"I know you're lonely. Especially after losing Jonathan."

Tears started to trickle down her cheeks. She nodded. "This isn't fair to me. I want a real marriage."

He hugged her, but she pulled away, still weeping.

"Ah, honey," he began.

She turned away. "I can't talk anymore. I'm going to take a shower. I have a meeting with my accountant."

He watched her figure retreat to the bedroom.

He took another drink, suddenly realizing he had an immense problem.

Fact was, he wouldn't have minded a divorce if it didn't mean losing all this — their lavish home, expensive sports cars, membership in the Montecito Country Club and their extravagant boats.

It hadn't always been like this. He'd made a name for himself in Vietnam, been somewhat of a hero.

Above the table, on the wall, was a laminated and framed picture of Mike on the cover of *Newsweek* magazine. He was dressed in green fatigues with a Stoner slung over his chest. On his forearm was a tattoo of a shark. "Shark Man of 'Nam," the caption read underneath his photo. "The meanest predator in the jungle."

Mike grinned. Everyone knew him in those days. Even the Viet Cong read *Newsweek* and put out a reward for his capture.

He recollected the incident that had brought him worldwide renown — a "body snatch" where the SEALs had been ordered to get a top ranking VC hiding out in a hootch down the river, bring him back to camp and question him.

After hours of trekking through swampy rainy terrain, the SEALs found the hootch. When the lieutenant signalled, one of the SEALs busted in the door.

Immediately, a real scared Viet Cong wearing black pajamas crashed through the hootch's nipa palm wall. Looking back over his shoulder, the VC ran straight into Mike.

Mike slammed his Stoner into the guy's balls, hit him in the back with his gun butt, rolled him on the ground and tied his hands.

Suddenly, he heard rounds of fire from outside the hootch. The SEALs retreated.

Even though the lieutenant yelled for him to leave the fucker and save his own skin, Mike dragged the VC behind him.

Mike considered his mission that evening just another "op." But the VC he captured was a biggie, one of the top men in the COSVN.

A television reporter stopped by the base to interview him. After that, there were other missions and wherever he went, the reporters covered him.

When he came back, he'd signed a book contract for $300,000. He was sought after by every production company in Hollywood. They paid top dollar.

But gradually, younger, more eager divers made their way into the business. There were no more book contracts. The production companies stopped calling.

He'd met Cathy when his career was going downhill. With his last funds and some help from Cathy, he'd started the dive business. Since then, her trust fund had been footing the bills.

Mike gazed at some photographs on an end table. One was a wedding picture of him and Cathy, dressed in a satin gown, studded with seed pearls. Her old man had put on some bash at the Four Seasons Hotel. It cost a small fortune.

Just to the right of their wedding picture was a photo of their son taken at age two. With his cropped blond hair and big blue eyes, Jonathan stared innocently out of his high chair.

He happened to glance at another picture of himself and his Navy buddy, Ed Hutton. Dressed in perfectly pressed Navy whites, Ed saluted him with a grin.

In truth, Mike had always felt closer to guys like Ed Hutton than he did to his wife or his deceased child. Perhaps that was unfeeling, callous and unenlightened. But in reality, he and his SEAL Team buddies had probably been through more than most husbands and wives go through in a lifetime.

He glanced away from the pictures. The present loomed, menacing and overwhelming.

Feeling strangely vulnerable, he waited forty-five minutes until Cathy had left the house and then picked up the phone and dialed.

A female voice answered.

"It's me," he said. "Meet me at the Radisson in an hour."

"Make it two," she said. "The kids have a soccer match in an hour. Then I'll be free."

Mike stirred a whiskey sour with his index finger. The ice cubes tinkled against the glass like wind chimes.

He opened the sliding glass door of his hotel room, and gazed down at the courtyard where royal palms surrounded a circular blue tiled pool.

Sunworshippers lounged in chairs beneath large beach umbrellas. Beyond the iron gates of the sun-drenched courtyard, he glimpsed the Santa Barbara Harbor and farther beyond, the glistening blue Pacific.

A light ocean breeze ruffled his sunbleached blond hair. He took a sip from his drink. He felt relaxed — his body sated with just the faintest dwindling tingle of lovemaking. He'd been coming to this hotel for almost a year with Lynn Connors and each time was always as good as the last.

A sudden whiff of French perfume and sweat met his nostrils, and he felt a tickle down the back of his spine, like the light stroke of butterfly wings.

He turned around to face Lynn, standing just behind him, tracing circles over his back with her fingertips. A sheer black slip was draped over her tanned shoulders.

He grabbed her fingers and kissed her hand. "Don't start, Lynn," he said. "We'll never get back in time."

He turned away from the courtyard and walked inside to the bedroom table.

He picked up his Rolex. It was almost four o'clock. They'd been in this hotel room all afternoon. Someone was bound to miss them. She had to get her kids. He had to give a dive lesson.

"Oh, Mike, we hardly see each other. Please, don't go." Her dark almond eyes pleaded with him.

He looked in her eyes shaded by thick lashes and felt a hunger, a craving pulling him right into her being.

"You have great muscles." She threw back a strand of long dark hair from her face, and traced her fingers over his shoulders, then down the gold fuzz of his chest.

He winked. "Not bad for a guy in his early fifties, huh?"

"I'd say pretty good for a twenty-year-old. How did you get to be such a hunk?"

Mike gazed at Lynn. He bent her face to his and kissed her softly on the mouth.

He felt her tongue flicker in and out. He groaned, sighed and gave in to the pressure of her mouth against his. He felt the warmth of her body, the velvety softness of her breasts and the round smoothness of her stomach. He lifted her slip and ran his fingers down her spine, stopping just short of the small mole at the crook of her back. He followed her back to the bed.

When it was over, they both lay in bed, exhausted. He watched a bead of perspiration drip down her forehead.

She smiled, and propping herself up on one elbow, kissed him lightly on the lips. He took a long look at her nude body beneath the sheets and slid his hand along her curves. She had a great set of knockers. Yes, Lynn was his kind of girl.

He'd met Lynn several years ago when Cathy had invited her and her husband, Buck, over to their house for a barbecue. Buck was a dentist and the couple had a nice home in Hope Ranch.

But Mike could tell Lynn wasn't satisfied with her lifestyle, especially after she had taken the guided tour of the Gallaghers' luxurious home in Montecito.

After Mike offered the couple drinks, Lynn made the comment, "We'll be moving to Montecito soon." Mike thought he detected a hint of envy in her eyes.

Buck looked startled and coughed.

Mike had the distinct impression that a dentist's income couldn't support a home like this in Montecito.

Lynn was a curvaceous, slim brunette wearing a Christian Dior sunback dress and strappy sandals.

Mike sized up Buck, an ordinary looking guy with dark reddish-brown hair, freckles and a slender frame built up by working out at a gym. He had on casual pants, a plaid shirt and a Navy SEAL baseball cap.

Mike guessed Lynn was the social climber. Her conversations revolved around the best restaurants in Santa
Barbara, the wineries of Solvang and the North Coast
and the activities of Hollywood's celebrities. Several times
during the evening, he caught her winking at him slyly.

He'd secretly thought about having an affair with Lynn,
but the Connors were friends, so he hadn't done it. Then
last year, he'd bumped into Lynn unexpectedly when her
husband was out of town, and they'd ended up in that
hotel room. She turned out to be a hell of a good time
and she did whatever he asked — in and out of bed.

Lynn idolized him. He felt young again. She reminded
him of better days, better times when he was a celebrity
and sought after by starlets — not like the present.

Their nights in the hotel rooms grew more frequent
until they were meeting once a week. He couldn't seem
to get enough of Lynn and then one day, he realized he
needed her.

Mike's affairs were usually brief with women from out
of town — not women in Santa Barbara, so close to his
wife. He knew what he was doing was dangerous, but he
couldn't stop.

"I wish we could be together more often," she said.

He kissed her forehead. "We can't, honey. Not now,
anyway."

"Then when?" she demanded.

"Give it some time."

She sat up in the bed, folded her arms and frowned.
"I don't like sneaking around like this," she pouted.

His voice grew firmer. "Lynn, we've been over this
before."

Mike rubbed his chin and frowned. He turned away,
got up from the bed and rummaged for his shorts in the
pile of clothes on the floor. He grabbed his shirt from the

back of a chair.

When he'd buttoned up his shirt, he turned to face Lynn. She was still pouting.

He sat next to her. He ran his fingers through her hair and stroked her head. "Ah, honey," he said. "You know I love you. I want to marry you, but I can't."

"Just divorce Cathy," she said emphatically.

He turned away from her. Several times, he'd been on the verge of telling Lynn about his financial situation. But he'd always been afraid she'd break it off with him. He figured that's why she was dissatisfied with Buck.

He held his breath, then spoke. "My finances aren't so good right now." He grimaced, waiting for her reaction.

"But what about your dive and travel business?"

"Look, I've lost a lot of money recently." That was only partially true.

"Don't tell me this," she said. "You're rolling in money. That's just an excuse."

He sat down on the bed and took her by the shoulders. "I'm afraid not."

She glared at him.

"You know I want you..." he began. Finally, he told her what had been on his mind all afternoon. "Cathy wants a separation...maybe a divorce."

Her eyes widened. "That's great!"

He shook his head. "But, I can't afford it. Not and give you what you want."

"Even if you got a divorce, you'd have enough," she argued. "That house alone must be worth four million."

He pursed his lips, paused, then spoke. "Cathy would get the house. She paid for it with her trust fund."

"She did what?"

"You heard me, Lynn. The house is Cathy's, not mine."

"Why didn't you tell me this before?" she said aghast.

He sighed. "I guess I didn't want to lose you."

"I don't believe you."

"It's true." He tapped her shoulder and lifted her face. His voice cracked. "I'm in love with you, Lynn. But it's not the right time."

She got up from the bed in fury. She turned her back on him and clenched her fists.

Well, he should have known it. At any rate, she'd been a good time.

Then she did something unexpected. She turned back around. She was weeping.

Mike got up from the bed, grabbed her and held her to his chest. She really must love him, not just the money. That was some small consolation. But, he knew love wouldn't be enough for Lynn, not for the long run.

"There must be some way..." Her eyes begged him for an answer, but there was none.

He shook his head and kissed her on the forehead.

Lynn turned away from him. She wiped her eyes. "Oh, God," she moaned. "What are we going to do?"

Mike sighed in desperation.

"I wish she were dead!" she cried, beating her fists against his chest.

Mike was surprised. He'd never seen Lynn this angry.

He got up from the bed again and went to put on his pants. He glanced over at her, but she was still sulking. He pursed his lips in frustration. "Oh, come on, you know you didn't mean that, did you?"

Lynn hung her head. But she didn't deny her feelings.

Gazing at Lynn, Mike had the same thought.

Several years ago, in addition to his own life insurance, they'd had to increase Cathy's, due to her heavy financing of their assets. It was about a million dollars.

With Cathy's trust fund and the insurance, he'd have enough.

What if she were dead?

CHAPTER

2

MIKE PULLED HIS SLEEK Betram 35 convertible sports fisher into the Santa Barbara Marina. He eased in beside a sports fisher with the name *Seahawk* painted in bold red across its white bow.

After tying up his boat, he helped his divers with their gear. They were finishing up their training for their NAUI certificates.

Once the last of the divers unloaded, he took a shower and changed clothes. He walked to the marina parking lot and transferred his gear to his car with a bumper sticker reading "I'd rather be diving."

The conversation with Cathy from the previous day still hung heavy on his mind.

He decided he needed a drink before heading out. He wandered over to Brophy Brothers and up the stairs to the bar.

Mike was a regular at Brophy's. Its veranda-bar offered an overview of the spacious marina with its numerous yachts, sailboats and fishing boats.

He made his way to the bar and took a stool. There were plenty of places open in the afternoon, especially on a weekday.

"Mike Gallagher! Good to see you, buddy." Tim, the bartender, slapped a menu on the bar in front of him. Tim had a big smile on his tan face.

Mike beamed. After all these years, most people in Santa Barbara knew Mike Gallagher. He still got a high out of being a celebrity.

Mike casually opened the menu. "A Michelob light and some fried clams."

Tim placed some silverware on the bar, walked over to the steins and returned moments later with the beer. "So how was Truk?"

"Couldn't be greater." Mike smiled and drank his beer.

"Any more trips planned?"

"Now that you ask, I'm headed out to Fiji for a month for a photo shoot with *National Geographic*. Imagine it, Tim — warm water, cold beer and hot women." He winked. "Why don't you come along?"

"Sounds like a great idea. Oh, what I wouldn't give for a month in Fiji!"

"So, pack your bags."

"Yeah, right," Tim answered sarcastically. "Our next vacation is to the mother-in-law's." Tim wrinkled his nose. "Ah! New Jersey! Grey skies, polluted air, chilly water and cold women." He shivered. "Paradise!"

Mike laughed and shook his head. "Yeah, well, the beer's still okay in Jersey. Anyway, we'll do it next time." Mike pointed his finger at Tim.

"You got a deal." Tim snapped his fingers. "Next time. You're one lucky guy, Mike."

Mike let the cool beer drizzle down his throat. Most people considered him lucky, and he wanted to keep it that way. He had an image to uphold. No one knew the truth except Lynn.

Tim brought his clams, slapping the plate down on the counter. "Did you hear about the two divers who drowned two weeks ago at Santa Cruz Island?"

Mike shook his head.

"It was in the *News-Press*. Front page article. You didn't see it?"

"I'm playing catch up from my trip. I haven't read a paper in days." He paused. "What did they do? Run out of air?"

"Yeah."

"Anyone we know?"

Tim shook his head. "Naw, they were from San Diego. Novices."

"The Channel Islands are no place for novices. Too many caves. Those mazes inside are killers."

Tim nodded. "I agree."

Mike ordered another beer, drinking in silence, while Tim went to help another customer.

Mike's eyes narrowed. From where he was sitting he could see the harbor and then farther on, the island of Santa Cruz — one of the five Channel Islands.

Suddenly, he remembered the cave.

March 1967...

He and Ed Hutton had taken some weekend liberty from the Naval Amphibious Base at Coronado and headed out to the Channel Islands for some spear fishing. It was a last opportunity for some fun before departing for 'Nam to hunt a different kind of game — "Charlie."

They'd anchored their sports fisher about twenty yards off the rugged cliffs of Santa Cruz. It was a sunny day — perfect for diving. The sea was calm. The light morning mist had burned off and the noon temperature was about seventy degrees.

It would be the last comfortable weather he'd see like that for a while. In a few weeks, he'd be sucking up river mud in tropical jungles.

"Hey, Mikey boy, how about giving me a hand with this gear?" Ed yelled from below deck. Ed was wearing swim trunks and a tee shirt that read "SEAL Team One — When You Care Enough to Send the Very Best" superimposed over a map of Vietnam. He flashed Mike a toothy grin.

Mike smiled. That wiry 170 pound body of Ed's packed the meanest punch in SEAL Team One, although no one would have guessed it. Some of the guys called Ed "Regs" because he did everything according to regulation — even sporting a crew cut when most of the guys wore their hair over their ears.

Mike threw back a strand of sunbleached hair and wiped his unshaven boyish face. He grabbed the forty-five pound tanks from his freckle-faced buddy as easily as if they were a couple of cans of beer.

Mike slipped the gold medallion from his neck and laid it on a nearby bench. He zipped his tight black neoprene suit over his broad chest, strapped a tank on his back, slipped on a mask, grabbed his fins and spear gun and jokingly threw his dive buddy a good-bye kiss.

"Hey, save that for your babes," Ed yelled.

Mike laughed. He couldn't see Ed, but suspected he was giving him the bird. He didn't have time to insult his buddy back. Taking a stride off the stern of the boat, he plunged fins first into the cool "Pacific blue" — like he'd done dozens of times in practice missions off San Nicholas and San Clemente.

For a moment, he felt his feet walk on pure nothingness, but almost instantly, the water hit him like a frigid arctic blast. He tried not to focus on the cold, knowing that within a few minutes, the water seeping into his wet suit would warm and he'd be insulated.

He heard Ed splash down behind him.

Mike gave Ed an okay signal and a thumbs-down. Ed returned the gesture and led the way. They swam down the anchor line and southwest from the placidly floating sports fisher. Descending through the lush submarine kelp forest, they held their spear guns close to their sides to remain as streamlined as possible and avoid entanglement in the sinuous leafy vines which rose toward the surface some twenty-five feet above the sand.

Mike's spear gun, his pride and joy, had cost a full week's pay, but was worth it. The weapon had a stainless steel shaft with folding wings and breakaway tips.

Ed touched Mike's arm and pointed in an easterly direction.

Mike squinted. Thirty feet in the distance, he made out the familiar humped shape and bright red band of a sheepshead. He was probably a good fifteen or twenty pounds. Excellent eating. But luring the fish in for the kill would be impossible without some chum.

The two divers spotted a patch of spiny purple sea urchins attached to a ledge along the wall. They swam to the ledge, took out their knives, broke open several of the urchins and began smashing them on the rocks.

Sheepshead were smart. It was uncanny. Mike had seen many a sheepshead come within range of a camera on a photo dive, but make for the depths as soon as a spear gun was visible. Mike knew the only way to kill the fish was to outsmart it.

After grinding up the urchins, Mike and Ed made their way to a large rock and hid behind it. They kept their spear guns well out of view and slowed their breathing. This was nothing new to either of them. In SEAL training, the two had learned how to sit for hours without moving a hair.

Almost immediately, small brown scavenging rockfish appeared from the island walls and swam toward the urchins. Then a few greedy garibaldi darted from the kelp and picked at the bait.

Cautiously, the sheepshead swam a little closer. Ed started to edge up, but Mike pressed his shoulder firmly. The sheepshead was fifteen yards away. He would come closer. Mike didn't want to spoil it by going too soon.

The sheepshead's approach was agonizingly slow. The fish was larger than Mike had previously guessed, probably about twenty-five pounds, a survivor of the water world. The fish moved in — ten feet, then five. Finally, it came in for the kill.

When the sheepshead was distracted with active feeding, Mike nodded.

Then Ed made his move. Carefully, he took the safety off and eased up slowly. He brought his gun up for a head shot and fired. The tip went straight through the tough plate of the sheepshead.

Mike clenched his fist and raised his arm in triumph. After flopping a few seconds, the quarry was still.

There was sudden terror in the water as the two divers became hunters. The hit sent the other fish darting off and scattering in all directions. The divers would have to find another spot for a second kill.

After driving the stringer under the sheepshead's gill plate and out the mouth, Ed removed the spear, then snapped the stringer on his belt.

The two moved into open water, away from the rock wall. Mike led the way. Above and behind him, Ed followed. His dangling fish left a faint trail of blood in its wake.

Abruptly, a dorsal-finned grey shape, about seven feet in length, appeared on the scene. Mike instantly recognized the intruder. A mako. It must have been cruising in the area and picked up the scent of blood.

The mako was mean-looking – an aggressive and ruthless shark armed with stiletto-sharp teeth. Luckily, makos were usually loners, but they were unpredictable predators.

Alarmed, Ed straightened up, pointed in the direction of the boat and gradually ascended to the surface.

The shark looked as if it were leaving and turned away from the two divers, but then circled around again, this time making a run past Ed.

Meanwhile the sheepshead, which was supposedly dead, quivered, spilling a puff of blood into the water.

The shark made an increasingly bold foray toward the divers. Quickly, Ed made a few kicks toward the shark and thrust aggressively forward with his gun.

The mako backed off, came around, then hovered in the water. After a few seconds, it dropped back to Ed's level and moved in a little closer.

Ed kicked again and made another feint with the gun. But, rather than backing off, the shark turned and swam directly toward him. He had to back-kick to avoid it.

Taking temptation out of reach of his body, Ed quickly unclipped the stringer. His dinner drifted downward into the blue abyss.

The mako turned and dove down like a jet fighter closing in on a wounded enemy craft. The fish was eaten in a flash.

The diversion gave Ed just enough time to surface, escaping the impending danger.

Now, the mako turned. The sheepshead was only an appetizer; the shark wanted a main course.

Mike thought about taking a shot at the mako, but shooting an animal that large might make it more aggressive. He looked up, gauging his distance from the boat. He didn't want to make a run for it. He'd never make it in time.

Mike wasn't the kind to back off from a fight. He decided to stand his ground.

The shark studied Mike, then made its move. It approached him and began to roll. Mike nailed it in the nose with the gun butt as hard as he could. The force of impact jarred his arm to the elbow. But, in no time, the shark had righted itself and was turning around to make another pass.

Mike looked around for some escape. Just to the right, along the ledge of the wall, he saw his chance — a yawning gap in the rock, perhaps twenty feet in width. There were numerous caves like these on the island, formed from faults in the volcanic shelf. If it was deep enough, he could get out of sight, and the shark might leave him alone. Large sharks rarely went into caves.

He swam toward the cavern, and with relief, passed through the threshold. He looked back at the shark. Its streamlined body was still circling.

Mike knew he would need to stay calm and conserve air. Glancing at his console, he noted 1,500 PSI, which at a shallow depth, would give him roughly another half-hour. He could make it back to the boat, if the shark gave up its search and left the area before then.

Cautiously, he turned on his dive light and shone it into the gaping hole. The chamber itself was larger than he thought — maybe fifty feet in width and height. It was sort of oval shaped. The jagged brown rock was chunky, formed from volcanic action mixed with layers of marine sedimentation. The floor was sandy with small ripple marks from the surge.

On one of the ledges, he made out the familiar shape of a brick red "bug" — a California spiny lobster. In fact, the ledges were loaded with bugs. Some perched on top of one another; some peeked out of the jagged rocks.

He shone his flashlight on the lobsters. Their luminescent eyes reflected the light.

He realized he'd made a mistake shining the flashlight directly at the bugs. The lobsters reacted in a split-second to the beam of light by making squeaking sounds with their antennae and scattering over the walls of the cave. Their movements flicked up the silt along the ledges.

The fine silt scattered like puffs of dust balls, reducing the visibility as mini-explosions billowed in the water around him. Hoping the bugs would settle down, Mike turned off the flashlight.

He waited an eternal few minutes. He glanced out of the cave. The mako was still darting back and forth.

Trying to get even farther away from the shark, he decided to swim to the back of the cave. He turned on his flashlight and made his way around the wall, covering a distance of approximately twenty-five feet.

His fin happened to brush the wall and almost landed on one of the bugs. It spooked, but instead of scuttling up the side of the cave, it disappeared backwards into the darkness.

Mike reached across the ledge where the lobster had been perched and flicked away some silt. The cave wasn't as shallow as he had originally surmised. Instead, a tunnel veered off from the original chamber — a dramatic fissure in the rock. He directed his light into the recess. The tunnel, about six feet in width and height, extended backward with no end in sight.

Inside the tunnel, the beam of light rolled over a familiar cylindrical shape. He did a double take. He hesitated for a moment, but he was intrigued. He knew he shouldn't be exploring a tunnel in a cave without a line, but he'd always been the daredevil of his unit.

Curious, he swam over the threshold into the blackness of the tunnel. The object was not that far from the entrance. He scraped away the silt and debris with the palm of his hand to discover a silver dive tank, in pretty good condition.

He brushed off one of the hoses holding the pressure gauge. The tank was empty. A queasy feeling built up in his stomach. Likely, the tank was attached to someone. Cautiously, he waved additional silt aside. It rose in murky clouds.

He waited for the silt to settle. Once the water had cleared, he looked down on a horrifying scene. Behind the dive mask was a mass of putrid flesh — the regulator still in what was left of the decaying lips.

Jesus! Startled, he dropped his flashlight. He'd never seen a corpse before and this thing was grotesque. He suspected the only thing holding the flesh in place was the mask and wet suit hood.

He caught himself gulping in the air from his regulator. He backed off for a moment and forced himself to breathe slowly, the way he'd learned to do it in SEAL training. His breathing became more regular. He recovered from the initial shock and picked up his flashlight.

He wondered how the poor bugger had managed to run out of air. As he shone the light into the tunnel, he saw the answer to his question. The tunnel branched into a dangerous labyrinth. The cave was a killer — a twisted maze that led into subterranean caverns.

There were dozens of caves like these in the Channel Islands. Often, novice divers, going out on a pleasure jaunt, would come upon them, decide to do a little exploring, maybe catch a few bugs. They'd neglect to take a line. Then, someone would silt up the chamber, head back into the maze, and attempting to find a way back, would panic, run out of air and die.

Mike glanced at his console. Shark or no shark, it was time to make his way back to the boat. In ten minutes, he would be out of air. He had no intention of ending up another victim of this labyrinth. He left the body where it was and headed to the main chamber.

When he reached the entrance to the cave, there was no sign of the shark. But he couldn't be sure, since makos had the habit of disappearing from a scene and reappearing right smack in your face.

He swam away from the island walls and into open water, then northeast towards the sports fisher. His finger rested lightly on the trigger of his spear gun as he moved upward through the kelp forests.

About five yards from the dive ladder, he hit the surface. He could see Ed at the railing. When Ed spotted him, he ran to the stern.

Mike felt a sense of instant relief as he put his foot on the step and his buddy helped him up.

"Damn, I was about to radio the Coast Guard," Ed said. "Tell them I had a dead body on my hands."

"Do I look like a dead body?" Mike asked, unstrapping his weight belt and tanks and pulling off his hood. He sank into a chair and grabbed a towel.

Ed studied him. "Naw, you look an ordinary hell-raising sailor to me."

Mike rubbed his head in the towel. "Speaking of dead bodies, I found one down there."

"Did I hear you right?"

Mike threw his towel on the chair. "You heard me, man. I saw a corpse down there."

"Where was it?"

"In this cave. I went in to get away from the mako. There were fingers branching out in all directions — like a maze. Some guy must have run out of air trying to find his way out."

"Oh shit. We gotta put in a report to the Coast Guard."

Mike felt a knot form in his stomach. "Ah, man! C'mon, Ed. Don't be a fucking fool." He realized he'd made a mistake mentioning the body.

Irritated, Mike dug his finger into Ed's chest. "Look, Regs, the sheriff's department will have us down at the station for hours. We'll be AWOL."

"Well, we just can't walk away and leave a dead body..." Ed began.

Mike stood his ground. "The hell we can't. We're going to be in deep shit if we report this incident. The plane leaves tomorrow at 1300. We're due back at the base. We've gotta get briefed and packed. We don't have time for this crap."

Ed rubbed his chin and shook his head. "I don't know, man. That poor bugger probably has relatives...."

"Suppose they keep us for questioning," Mike argued. "You want to be sitting in the police station, answering questions about some dead body while the rest of the guys are crouched in a Navy slick ready to jump into the jungle?"

Mike took a long hard look at Ed. He knew Ed wanted to go to 'Nam just as much as the other SEALs. "C'mon, Ed," Mike urged. "We got a job to do out there."

Ed leaned against the railing and stared into the water.

Mike whispered in his ear. "We're part of a team."

Ed hesitated. "Oh, hell," he muttered. "Screw the body. Let's go to 'Nam."

"Yeah!" Mike shouted. "Fun, excitement, life in the mud!"

"HOOYAH!" Ed hollered, raising the SEAL Team cry. "Let's do it, Shark Man."

Mike grinned. The name Shark Man seemed to fit. He laughed and feigned a punch at Ed. "All right, let's kick some ass! Let's shoot Charlie!" He switched on the portable radio. It was playing the Beach Boys, "Round, Round Get Around, I Get Around."

Forget about it, Mike, just forget about it, he muttered to himself as he started back to the stateroom to change.

Afterwards, he and Ed made a solemn vow never to tell anyone about the cave or the body, although the shark story had been embellished into a hand-to-hand combat with a great white.

Odd, how that body had faded from his memory...until now.

Would it be murder, he found himself wondering, if someone were to get lost in those caves and run out of air? Or would it be just another dive accident?

CHAPTER

3

"YOU OKAY?" SUSAN ASKED. "You look a little pale."

Cathy glanced up at their new assistant, a perky redhead they had hired a month ago.

"I'm fine, Susan." Cathy checked the time. "I'm meeting Dad for lunch. Watch the shop while I'm gone, will you?"

Susan nodded reassuringly. "Sure thing."

Cathy turned back to gaze at the dive shop located in the hub of downtown Santa Barbara. The front window was decorated with drapes of fishnets studded with dried starfish set against a cardboard backdrop of palm trees lining a deserted beach. Posters for exotic destinations — Cozumel, Malaysia and Australia — lined the walls. Fluorescent colored skin suits and masks hung from the side walls, and in the back were the tanks marked with yellow crosses for nitrogen-oxygen mixtures. Behind the glass-enclosed main counter were regulators and consoles, gauges, computers, high-intensity lights and line reels.

Cathy opened the door and a gust of wind blew a

strand of hair back from her face. She heard the shrieks
of sea gulls overhead.

As she approached Cabrillo Boulevard, a bicycler
wheeled past her, and then a couple of teenage girls
skated by on rollerblades. She came to the intersection of
Cabrillo and State Street and quickly passed the Dolphin
Fountain.

She stepped onto the rickety wooden planks of Stearns
Wharf and immediately spotted an old friend, Buck
Connors, walking out of the Santa Barbara Shellfish Com-
pany with a white cardboard box under his arm.

Buck, dressed in a cotton shirt, jeans and sandals,
hardly looked the part of a dentist. If he had longer hair,
he could have been mistaken for one of the faded middle-
aged hippies that milled around the harbor. He had a
lively step to his walk.

"Hey, Cathy!" Buck exclaimed, his green eyes twin-
kling behind gold framed glasses. "Long time, no see. Is
your beach bum of a husband back from overseas?"

She smiled. "Mike just got back a couple of days
ago, Buck."

Buck was her dentist — a root canal specialist. Gradually, they'd become friends and in exchange for passing
along Mike's business card to his colleagues, the
Gallaghers had introduced the Connors to the dive community and invited them aboard their boat for outings.

Cathy and Buck shared an enthusiasm for underwater
photography.

Cathy glanced at the package he was carrying. "Buying seafood?"

"Yep. But I sure wish I were diving for it. My freezer's
getting a little low these days."

Cathy grinned. That was a hint if ever she heard one.
Buck always wanted to go diving. Now that it was No-

vember, the season for lobster hunting in California, she knew Buck was expecting another trip. "Well, now that Mike's back, maybe we'll be doing some bug hunting soon," she said.

"Oh, yeah!" Buck said enthusiastically.

"I promise we'll take you out next time we go." She owed Buck one. Only recently, Buck had cancelled a complimentary golf vacation to take care of an emergency impacted tooth of hers that had become infected. To repay him, she'd offered to take him out on their next dive trip.

"That's great! I'm gonna hold you to it. Too bad Mike's not home more often," he said wistfully. "I could get in a lot more trips."

"Believe me, I feel the same way. I'm tired of him being gone all the time." She sighed and stared out at the ocean.

"I was gone a lot when I was in the Navy. Jeez, I was only married six months when I was shipped overseas. Love, marriage, and I'm off on a Mediterranean cruise. It was pretty rough on both of us."

Cathy nodded. "It is rough," she said, careful to not reveal too much about her present state of mind.

"Yep. Well, you take it easy, Cathy."

"You too, Buck. We'll be in touch soon."

She waved good-bye to him, and then headed to The Harbor Restaurant. Built right off the wharf on wooden pilings, it was considered one of the best restaurants on the pier.

As Cathy opened the wooden door, she heard the chattering of diners and caught a whiff of cooking seafood and steaks.

The hostess recognized her immediately. "Cathy, your father's waiting for you. Follow me."

She led Cathy through the dining room decorated with built-in boxes of tropical plants and model sailboats. Along the walls were glass enclosed sketches of Santa Barbara's waterfront in the 1920s when the restaurant was a yacht club — a picturesque view of Castle Rock in 1892, a floral parade honoring the Great White Fleet, fishermen displaying marlin. They stopped at a window table across from a large aquarium filled with tropical fish.

"How's my girl?" Her father's tanned face was weather-beaten by sun and wind.

Cathy flashed him one of her perky smiles, but her voice faltered. "I'm fine, Dad."

"It doesn't sound that way."

Cathy ignored his comment. She took a seat and ordered from a blond waiter who was dressed in an Hawaiian shirt and standing beside them.

Her father handed the waiter his menu. "I'll have the usual."

The waiter nodded. Most people in Santa Barbara knew Cathy's father and he frequented this restaurant. James T. Chesterfield was a successful commercial real estate developer.

Cathy gazed out at the harbor dotted with yachts and sailboats. The carefree atmosphere contrasted sharply with her mood. She bit her lip anxiously.

"You're awfully quiet today," her father said. "Anything bothering you?"

Cathy lowered her eyes. "No, I'm just worried about the dive business."

"So, tell that husband of yours to get a real job."

"I wish it were as simple as that. But, you know Mike. I can't see him punching a clock."

Her father wrinkled his brow. "I've never understood why you married him. You could have had any man in

Santa Barbara and you chose a damned sailor."

Cathy pursed her lips. Her father had seen all those women in bikinis hanging around the dive shop and flirting with Mike. He'd immediately pegged Mike as a womanizer. The two had never gotten along.

Shortly after her graduation from Stanford, Cathy had fallen in love with Mike and married him.

She'd met him at a charity function given in Santa Barbara for the Save the Whales Society. It was a Caribbean style luncheon, followed by swimming and dancing, held aboard a yacht.

She was talking with a group of friends and sipping champagne when she noticed several guests pointing at the sky. She shaded her eyes, glanced up and recognized the shape of a descending parachutist.

She thought it was someone from the Naval Special Warfare Station going through a training exercise on one of the nearby Channel Islands. But as he dropped, she realized he was directly overhead, destined to land on their boat.

In seconds, the man plummeted out of the sky directly in front of her.

She jumped out of the way as his chute billowed out and knocked champagne bottles off several tables.

Incredulous, she approached him. He was a muscular blond with a drop-dead smile and Hollywood good looks, dressed in a black wet suit under his parachute harness.

"Do you often drop in unexpectedly on private parties?" she asked.

He burst into laughter as he gathered up the canopy.

The other guests on board the yacht applauded and then went back to their drinks and chitchat.

One of her friends, Bob Evans, who had been in the

Navy, stood up from the table and pounded him on the back. "Cathy, meet Mike Gallagher, Shark Man of 'Nam, former leader of SEAL Team One. He's one tough hombre."

"Cathy Chesterfield." She laughed, shaking his hand. "I wish I had my camera. Your arrival would have made a great shot."

"Cathy's an underwater photographer," Bob said. "She's just opened up her own studio here in Santa Barbara. You should get her to take some pictures of you, Mike."

"I just might do that," Mike answered.

"That's a hell of a way to crash a party," she commented, as he folded up his chute.

"Mike's one of the celebrities here today," Bob said. "He's in a new film to be released by Paramount. They thought this jump would be good publicity."

"I'll make a point to see the film," she added.

She realized she'd seen his picture. Mike proved to be as attractive in person as in his photographs. "Weren't you on the cover of *Newsweek*?" she asked.

Mike smiled. "That's me."

"Yeah, Mike's a hot shot, Cathy," Bob said, pulling out a couple of chairs for them at a nearby table and motioning for them to sit down. "He's really special. Damn few people could do what he did in 'Nam. Top secret stuff. Hell, he was a hero. He's got three rows of medals. This guy's the best. Just beware. The women have the hots for him. He has to literally fight them off."

"I hope not with an M-16," Cathy said.

Mike laughed. She immediately fell in love with his laugh — deep and rich, yet boyish.

After that, he asked her to take a couple of pictures of him on some underwater dive expeditions and before she knew it, they were dating.

At first their relationship was extremely physical. She took great pleasure in watching his lower torso in his swim trunks from behind. Sometimes, when they were preparing for a sailing trip, she'd watch his strong arms getting sails on deck, and she'd walk right up behind him and whisper something provocative in his ear. Before he could finish bringing up the sails, they'd be down on the deck making love, their trip forgotten in the heat of passion.

Later, their relationship developed into something more. Some of the best times in her life were when she went on underwater dives with him. He'd show her spots for underwater photography, places the tourists often missed. Her photos began to win awards.

Cathy's mind returned to the present. "I guess I just fell in love with him, Dad," she said.

Her father leaned back in his chair. "You know, I was a millionaire by the time I was fifty. Tell me, what pays for that fancy boat of his and the house? My trust fund?"

Cathy blushed. She didn't feel comfortable discussing finances with her father.

"Money isn't everything," she said quietly.

"It's a damned lot," her father argued, pushing back his chair.

"Dad, he was a top Navy SEAL!"

"Navy SEAL! He was a trained killer!"

"Now, Dad, that's not fair," she shot back. "You were a veteran."

"Korea was different." Her father folded his arms.

Cathy sighed. Arguing was pointless. Her father was used to getting his own way.

"Look, Cathy. I didn't give you a trust fund to throw away on that husband of yours. What are you going to do when the money runs out?"

She shrugged. "I don't know."

"If he loves you, he'll sell the business and find an-other job." Her father leaned back in his chair and stared at her. "If not, I'd divorce him."

"But we've been together for fifteen years!"

"So, that's no reason to stay together. Plenty of people get divorced after years of marriage." Her father pursed his lips. "He's not having another affair, is he?"

She shook her head. She avoided her father's eyes. Two years ago, she'd found out about a short-term affair Mike had in the Solomon Islands. She'd been tempted to divorce him then, but he'd been so apologetic, she'd reconsidered. Now the trips made her jittery.

These days, Mike was always traveling to some ex-otic overseas resort. Plenty of little brown-eyed women in those native villages would be all too willing to put out for a hotshot with a couple of hundred in his wallet. Not to mention the women in the bars who came onto him when he went drinking with the guys.

At first, she had accompanied Mike on their trips. Gradually, she'd gotten so wrapped up in his business, she didn't have time for her photography. Finally, she closed her shop.

But when she'd had Jonathan seven years ago, she'd stopped going overseas. She wanted to be at home with her child.

Last year, Jonathan had been taken away unexpect-edly. Just a fall from a monkey bar in a park. He'd hit his head on a piece of metal. He'd died almost instantly.

She'd thought about having another child. But she didn't think now was the right time, not with so many doubts about their marriage.

She still loved Mike. But sometimes, she had the feeling he cared only for her money. All that money was a hard thing for Mike to walk away from.

But how about her? Could she walk away from a man she had loved all these years?

Her father put his hands on the table and leaned forward. "Why don't you get a divorce? You're only thirty-eight. You can start over."

She frowned. She didn't like admitting her father might have been right about Mike. "Actually, I've suggested a separation."

Her father beamed. "I think you'll be a lot happier after a divorce."

"I didn't say a divorce. I said a separation."

"Same thing. Have you got a lawyer?"

Cathy shook her head.

He leaned over the table. "Well, why don't you give my attorney, Ron Carland, a call? He'll put you in touch with someone. You're going to need some advice."

She fingered the Perrier. "I don't know whether I need advice. I just need a little time to think things over."

"Everybody needs advice," her father said. "After all, you don't know how Mike will react. It's better to have someone looking out for your interests."

"I don't think Mike would do anything to deliberately hurt me."

"You just don't know. You always think the best of others. But people can be vicious."

Cathy glanced away from her father. She did have a tendency to overlook the bad in people. Plus, her husband could be just as stubborn and hardheaded as her father.

"Well, you do what you think is right," her father said. "Don't say I didn't warn you. The food's here."

Cathy looked up as the waiter placed the shrimp salad

in front of her and the grilled mahi-mahi in front of her
father.

Her father took a bite of the mahi-mahi, then spoke.
"What did you ever see in Mike?"

Cathy hesitated. "Actually, he's a lot like you, Dad.
Although you wouldn't care to admit it."

He raised his eyebrow. "Don't compare that dead-
beat husband of yours to me."

Cathy gave up arguing. She picked up her fork. Her
gold wedding ring glinted in the noonday sun. When
Mike had placed that ring on her finger, she had such an
incredible confidence in their love, she never thought they
could lose it. Yet now, she wasn't so sure.

When he got home, Mike poured himself another drink
from the bar. His throat was dry, parched. As he raised
the glass to his lips, his hands were trembling.

Actually, it wasn't the first time he had planned to kill.
While serving as a SEAL, one of his instructors had termed
all the ambush killings he went on as nothing but "pre-
meditated murder." But all those VC had been nameless
strangers. Cathy was his wife. He had loved her, slept in
the same bed with her.

He walked into the bedroom with the drink. He heard
his wife in the shower. He sat down on the bed and glanced
around the room.

On the wall were photos Cathy had taken when she
had been dating Mike. One was of Mike pointing to a
coral reef covered with rose anemones, another of Mike
diving through a veil of silvery blue mackerel glittering
like raindrops. Both had won awards.

He remembered the day he'd met her on the yacht,
when she was wearing a bathing suit wrap with daring
slits up the side. She was the most gorgeous and exciting

woman he'd ever met — not like the little Hollywood startlets he usually dated.

On their dive trips together, he used to get a kick out of watching her slowly unzip her sexy black neoprene suit and shake loose her long wet strands of hair. She was the only woman he had ever met that could dive better than his SEAL Team buddies.

She was a great promoter of his business. Her underwater photos of him were featured in all the dive magazines. Plus, she knew everyone in Santa Barbara. All she had to do was throw a few parties, drop some names, and before he knew it, he was swamped with requests for dive trips. Mike found the jet set would pay lavishly for the opportunity to dive, especially with a celebrity.

Only these days, he was no longer a celebrity.

For a moment he was filled with self-loathing.

But he knew he couldn't let emotion get in the way. There was no room for introspection. After all these years, he couldn't change his lifestyle. It was either him or Cathy. The way Mike saw it, this was war.

He heard the bathroom door open. He looked up to find Cathy standing in the bedroom, drying her hair. A white terry cloth towel was draped around her body. He could tell she was still upset, because there were tears dripping down her cheeks.

Glancing at Cathy, now drying her eyes with some tissues, he didn't think she was really convinced about the divorce. She still loved him. She was just angry over his constant trips.

He knew he had to say something to calm her down, stop her from proceeding too quickly with her plans. He took a sip of scotch and put the glass on an end table. "Cathy," he began. "I've thought about what you've said."

"Yes?" She turned around to face him.

"And you're right, honey. I have been gone a lot lately. We haven't really seen each other in a month. My trips overseas just seem to get longer and longer."

"Too long," she said, looking at the floor and putting aside the tissue.

"I know, hon," he agreed. "It's not fair to you."

Her eyes widened. "That's a surprise!"

"But, you're right. You can't have a marriage if one partner is gone all the time."

She looked startled. "I can't believe you're saying this, Mike. I've tried to tell you this for years. Did I have to threaten a separation before you'd finally take me seriously?"

"Maybe." He paused, trying to think up some excuse to win her back. "But, as a matter of fact, an old Navy buddy of mine called me up yesterday. He needs a dive trainer right here in Santa Barbara. The government's got a contract with him. I think I'll accept it, Cathy," he lied. "That would put me at home for at least a year. Meanwhile, why don't you get those papers ready to sell the business."

Her face glowed. She dried her eyes. "Mike, that would be fantastic!"

He walked toward her and gave her a hug. "Why don't we take a little break together?"

"What do you have in mind?" she asked.

"Why not a dive trip to Santa Cruz? Just the two of us. You've been by yourself too much. We can sunbathe, catch a few bugs, have a great time."

"Well, maybe..."

"Ah, come on, Cathy. You're the one who's been complaining about not being together. And if you still feel the same way, we can get that separation. But, I hope you'll change your mind." He kissed her softly on the lips.

She hesitated.

"Do it for us, Cathy," he said.

"All right," she finally agreed. "We haven't spent a whole weekend together in ages."

He tapped her on the chin. "That's my girl."

She smiled. "The vis has been great for diving."

"Great. We'll make it this weekend. The *Trident's* handling like a dream." He gave her another hug. "Why don't you make a run to the supermarket tomorrow. Get a few beers, some fruit for breakfast. But, don't get too much for dinner, " he added. "I've found a great place for bugs. This cave is loaded with them. We'll have lobsters for a month."

Hopefully, she gazed into his eyes. "Maybe things can be different for us."

He squeezed her hand and smiled. "I know they can."

CHAPTER

4

THE OCEAN WAS GLASSY — hardly a swell. Buck could see the sun setting on the horizon like a long, slow fire. In the marina, brilliant crimson rays silhouetted the swaying masts of sailboats. He gazed at the island of Santa Cruz rising from a crystal blue sea, and further to the north, Santa Rosa.

Buck parked his car in the designated lot next to the marina and took a stroll up the concrete breakwater lined with colorful pennants. He inhaled the waterfront smells — cooking crabs, diesel fuel, salt air. His eyes searched the numerous yachts, sailboats and sports fishers in the marina for Mike and Cathy's boat, the *Trident*. Just maybe they'd be planning on a run out to one of the Channel Islands.

Buck sighted the Gallaghers' sleek Betram 35 convertible. It was a classic sports fisher with a big fishing cockpit and teak interior, a single stateroom layout and thirteen feet of beam. It had a Bimini top over the flybridge and a lower helm in the salon. With its twin gas engines, it could reach thirty knots when running wide open. Mike had the SEAL Team slogan posted inside the salon. "The only easy day was yesterday."

Buck saw Cathy, dressed in cutoff jeans, tee shirt and tennis shoes. She was cleaning the deck. Most people would have never thought she was worth a fortune. But most "Santa Barbarians," as Buck sometimes jokingly termed the locals, were like Cathy — laid-back and casual. She waved and flashed him one of her gorgeous smiles. Mike had really lucked up marrying Cathy. She would have stopped all the men on the walkway, if she hadn't been with Mike.

"Hey, Buck," Cathy yelled.

"Is that Buck Connors?" floated Mike's voice from below. "Give me a hand with these tanks, will you, Doc?"

Buck snatched two tanks beside the boat and stepped onto the cockpit deck.

Mike emerged from the engine room, wiping his hands with an oily rag.

Buck and Mike went back a long way. They'd swapped tales about the Navy, played many a round of golf, and managed to sip more scotch-on-the-rocks at The Chart House than Buck cared to remember.

Mike broke into a smile, revealing just a hint of creases at the corners of his eyes. "Miller time!"

Hand it to a former SEAL to go for the liquid, Buck thought.

Mike went to get some beers out of the fridge. When he came back, he handed one to Buck and another to Cathy. Buck popped the top on his Miller and took a long, hard swallow. He gazed out at the ocean. "Pretty flat. Going out this weekend?"

Cathy leaned against the flybridge ladder and took a sip of beer. She wiped her forehead with her hand. "Yeah.

Divers say the vis is sixty feet."

"Where are you headed?"

"Santa Cruz. Mike's found a new place for bugs. He says there's so many, we'll be eating lobsters for a month."

"So, when's your next overseas expedition?" Buck asked, glancing at Mike.

"We hope not for awhile," said Cathy.

Buck felt a pang of sympathy for her. Buck often felt Mike could be a little more attentive to Cathy, and he'd said a few words to him, although he didn't press it. He wasn't the kind of person to get involved in other people's private relationships, unless it was requested.

"Actually, Mike's going to be home for awhile," Cathy piped up. "He's got a contract in Santa Barbara."

"That's great news! So..." Buck paused. "Is that invite still open, Cathy?" He remembered her promise to take him out on their next trip. Cathy always kept her word.

Cathy paused for a moment, looking as if she were struggling with some issue, but then broke into a smile. "Well, sure, Buck, why not? Hey, you and Lynn plan on coming along, too. Let's make a weekend of it."

Mike interrupted. "Buck has a busy practice, Cathy. He just can't drop everything on the spot."

Buck had a late morning tee time, but diving always won over golf. "Well, as a matter of fact, I'm free Friday. As far as I know, so's Lynn."

"Then it's settled," Cathy said.

"Great!" Buck responded. He wondering fleetingly why Cathy and Mike had hesitated, but dismissed it. "What can I bring?"

"Well, we're a little short on beer," Cathy said.

"I'll bring a cooler full."

Mike set his face firmly. "You and Lynn get your butts down here early," he ordered. "We shove off at 0800

Friday."

"Aye, aye, Captain." Buck gave him a snappy Navy salute.

"Aye, aye, Captain, sir," Cathy emphasized.

Buck chuckled. He drained his beer. He and Lynn were in for a treat. He'd get Rosa to watch the kids for the weekend. He crushed the beer can in his fist and tossed it in a nearby trash container on the wharf. He gave the couple a wave, turned and headed out to his car.

Buck pulled his Audi into the extended driveway of his home in Hope Ranch and parked beside Lynn's Lexus. His wife had just got the Lexus last year. Her previous car was only three years old, yet she considered it too shabby and insisted on a new one.

Rosa, the Hispanic maid who often doubled as a baby-sitter, was on her way out as he walked in. Her slightly plump figure was dressed in a bright flowered skirt and she wore a red bandanna wrapped around her glossy black hair. A large cross dangled around her neck.

"*Buenas tardes, Rosa,*" said Buck.

"*Buenas tardes, Señor Connors,*" she answered him, her lips breaking into a full smile against her mulatto skin.

Buck had lived in Spain when he was a teenager. He often spoke Spanish to Rosa.

"*Fui a la iglesia por el Dia de los muertos. Fue usted?*" she asked.

Buck shook his head. "*Tu sabes de que yo no voy a la iglesia, Rosa.*"

Buck had been born Catholic and Rosa always admonished him for not going to church. It was one of the little things he put up with for having the privilege of her help in the house. He couldn't quite figure out her brand of Catholicism, since she believed in all the Saints plus a conglomeration of minor spirits.

"*Le he estado diciendo que los espiritus malos van a agarrario si usted no va, Señor Connors,*" she scolded.

"*Rosa, tus espiritus malos son puro cuento.*"

Rosa warned him the evil spirits would get him, but Buck ignored her. He waved off her warnings good-naturedly as she left the house.

He walked through the kitchen and into the den. His sons, Scott and Kevin, were watching a rerun of a Star Wars movie. Kevin, the six year old, arms outstretched, ran up to greet him with a big hug.

"Hey, Dad," shouted Scott, his eight-year old, from across the room. "Tryouts went great. I made the team."

"Atta boy, tiger," Buck said, approaching his older boy with a high five. "Where's your mother?"

"Upstairs. Getting ready for a Junior League meeting."

"Oh, yeah." Thursday was another one of her nights out. She seemed more interested in improving their prestige than anything — often to the detriment of the kids' emotional well-being. He had wanted her to help build a place in the community, but he wondered if the children were getting the attention they needed from their mother.

"It's spaghetti night, right, Dad?" Scott said, interrupting his thoughts.

"Right." Buck remembered it was his night to fix dinner. "Just let me get changed, okay guys?"

"Spaghetti night! Spaghetti night!" Kevin yelled enthusiastically.

Buck gave his youngest a big smile and a pat on the back. "You've got it, son." He always tried to pay a lot of attention to his boys. He wanted them to have a stable upbringing, perhaps because he hadn't had one.

Buck made his way upstairs. He found his wife sitting at her vanity table in the bedroom. He looked around. Shirts that needed to be ironed were piled on a bedroom chair, and shoes and dresses were strewn about the room. Even with Rosa's visits three times a week, the house was still in disarray.

"Hi," he said, as he crossed the room and gave his wife a kiss on her slightly flushed cheek. Her skin felt warm against his mouth.

"Oh, I didn't hear you come in," she said absently, barely noticing his kiss.

He sighed. These days, it seemed his lovemaking skills were unappreciated. It hadn't always been this way. In his younger years, Lynn could hardly wait to have him inside her — gripping him tightly and arching her back in ecstasy.

Lynn was so pleased with him then, she dubbed him the "canal master." He smiled at her little joke. He liked being told he was good in the sack.

At first, he and Lynn had been extremely close. When they slept together, he would reach over to her and snuggle up, fitting her body against his chest, tucking his arm around her breasts, unable to let her go even in his sleep. They'd wake up together in the morning, still in each other's arms.

But now, sometimes, he'd wake up in the middle of the night, and reach over and the space in the bed would be empty. He'd get up, put on his bathrobe and wander around the house until he'd find her. She'd be in the living room watching TV, or in the den, reading a book.

"What are you doing?" he'd ask.

"I couldn't sleep."

"Come back to bed." He'd lead her tenderly by the elbow, back into the bedroom. "I need you beside me."

She'd follow him back, but she'd toss and turn in bed. Finally, hours later, they'd get to sleep.

Now, he watched her slipping into her white cotton dress. His eyes slid slowly down the front of her dress, over her full breasts and the curve of her hips, down to the outline of her trim thighs, barely visible beneath the flowing cloth.

Staring at her, he felt a growing sexual hunger in his groin. They hadn't made love in several weeks.

"Could you help me with this dress?" she asked, turning away from his stare.

"Sure." He stood behind her, as she held her shoulder-length dark hair up for him to button the dress in the back. Her tanned shoulders, moist and glowing against the white fabric, invited sexual passion. She smelled of expensive scent, musky and erotic.

He wished he were unbuttoning the dress. He kissed her softly on the nape of her neck. "Do you have to go, Lynn?" he asked. "You smell really good, honey. Too good not to go to bed with."

"Really, Buck," she answered, frowning and pulling away from him. "I'll be home by ten o'clock. I hardly have time to get out anymore."

He finished with the dress. He guessed it was new, because he hadn't seen it before. In the past year, she'd started going on weekend shopping sprees. She'd bought a whole closetful of dresses and a bureau of lingerie.

During the first years of their marriage, Lynn had been extremely careful with their budget. But over the years, after he had established a practice, she began to charge more and more on his credit cards.

Even this lavish home in Hope Ranch had been her idea. He complied with her request, although he really couldn't afford it.

Lynn had joined every club in Santa Barbara. She threw herself into the organizational whirlpool, volunteering for any and everything, moving up quickly to become treasurer or president.

Buck supposed he had encouraged Lynn in her role as a social climber. He needed a wife who could mingle well with the affluent, because he wanted referrals from other doctors and dentists.

But Lynn's demands were putting a burden on his bank account. He had a negative cash flow on some of his investment property, and it seemed like every month, he barely had enough to make his home mortgage, the car payments and the overhead of his luxurious dental office.

"Honey," he began. "I saw the Gallaghers at the marina. They asked us out on a dive trip for this weekend. It would be nice to get away for awhile, wouldn't it?" Lynn didn't dive, but sometimes she went on the dive trips with the Gallaghers. She'd sit on deck and read and sunbathe. The trips gave them both time to relax, and Lynn usually was more sexually responsive to him later.

She turned her classically oval face to him. "I was thinking more of Hawaii."

"Well, I don't have the time now for Hawaii." He pulled his hand away. "Or the money."

"You promised we'd go to Hawaii soon," she argued.

"Well, we'll see, Lynn." He patted her hand. "Right now, a dive vacation would be nice."

"I have plans," she answered quickly.

"You know Cathy likes having you along."

She shook her head firmly. "I don't want to go."

"Why not? You love spending time with the Gallaghers."

"I just don't want to go," she pouted. She sat down at the vanity table and picked up her lipstick, tracing the outline of her lips.

He felt frustrated. "C'mon, honey, this will give us a chance for a little vacation. We both need to get away." He sat beside her and stroked her dark hair. "Anyway, we haven't been alone together without the kids in ages."

"Anything could happen," she sulked. "Suppose there's a storm."

He threw up his hands. "Sweetheart, they're predicting clear skies tomorrow. The weather's perfect. C'mon, Lynn," he said, edging closer to her. "We'll have a great time."

She slammed her lipstick on the vanity table. "There was a diving accident reported in the Sunday paper. Two divers killed."

"They were novices," he replied. "They probably didn't know what they were getting into. Besides, Mike's a NAUI instructor and I have more than 200 dives under my belt."

She paused. She picked up her eyebrow pencil and began coloring her brows. She looked as if she were thinking up another line of attack. "You know there are sharks in the area. I worry."

"What — about sharks? How many divers have been killed by sharks?"

She shrugged. "Suppose you run out of air."

"Hah!" He paused. "Look. I've already told them we'd go."

"Well, just don't blame me if something goes wrong."

"Nothing's going to go wrong."

She glared at him again and put the finishing touches on her makeup. She gave her hair a few strokes with her brush, snapped on some sandals and walked out of the room. He had the urge to follow as he heard her heels clicking down the stairs, but he remembered the kids. They were hungry.

He caught another whiff of her perfume. He had the sudden feeling that it was just a little too sensuous for a night out with the girls.

He entered the bathroom and looked around. It was a mess — pantyhose drying on the racks and a wet towel on the floor.

He glanced at the glass-enclosed photographs on the wall — memorabilia from his many dive trips. He'd become adept at underwater photography over the years. Some of his photographs had won awards. There was a picture of a pale white anemone with a Caribbean cleaner shrimp caught in its tendrils; another of an orange and purple Spanish shawl nudibranch; and a third of a purple gorgonian, its lacy arms bent back by the surge. Macro-photography had become his special interest, and his eye for meticulous detail had served him well.

He undressed and took a quick shower before dinner. He was feeling more than a little upset with Lynn. It seemed she had an argument for everything these days. He shrugged off her objections, thinking of blue skies and sun and a great lobster dinner aboard the Gallaghers' boat.

CHAPTER

5

MIKE FELT THE WARMTH of the sun hitting his face. He cracked his eyelids and turned over in bed.

His wife lay sprawled beside him, the curve of her back against his chest. Her long blonde hair cascaded down the pillow and spilled over the side of the bed.

For a moment, he listened to her soft breathing. He glanced at her breasts and hips beneath the sheets, but he turned away.

It wasn't the first time he had turned away from those curves. He hadn't felt like a man with Cathy in several years.

But then, he supposed Cathy didn't feel like a woman with him. In their early days, she'd climb on top of him, whisper something provocative, flick her tongue in his ear, thrust back her golden hair, and close her sparkling green eyes, totally oblivious to the world. When it was over, she'd collapse from exhaustion against his shoulders, too tired even to roll over. She was asleep before he could release her from his arms.

She was the only woman he'd ever found who could keep up with him in and out of bed.

But, sadly enough, time had gone by, and he and Cathy had grown apart.

Determined, Mike rose quietly out of the bed so as not to disturb his wife's sleep. He walked into the bathroom to shower and shave, and dressed quickly. It was six o'clock in the morning.

Already, boats were beginning to leave the marina. If he hurried, he could make a run out to Santa Cruz Island and still be back in time for his two o'clock group of NAUI trainees. He needed to check out that cave.

Could he actually kill her? The question pierced him like a giant fishhook right through his heart.

Suppose the police found her body? He would be called down to identify it. Glancing at his wife, her cheeks slightly flushed in the early morning light, he had a hard time picturing her dead. Cathy was always so vibrant and alive. After a day in the morgue, she would be cold, stiff and white.

Suppose the police didn't find her until weeks or months later. Cathy was a beautiful woman. The corpse he had originally found in that cave years ago was grotesque. Would she look like that corpse?

Actually, there was a good chance that he wouldn't have to identify Cathy's body. The tunnels in that cave were so deep and so complicated that the police could search for weeks and never find anyone. With all that heavy scuba gear, her body could be buried forever under feet of silt.

Anyway, he had no more time to speculate about his wife's death. His hands automatically reached for the car keys, and his legs took him out the door.

He didn't know what he would do about Buck and

Lynn. He hadn't expected Cathy to invite them along. That was an added complication, but still, one he figured he could handle.

At the marina, Mike turned his mind to the task at hand. He unfastened the *Trident's* lines from the dock, started the engines and eased the boat into open water.

When he reached the island an hour and a half later, he dropped anchor. Then he geared up, lowered his face mask and plunged into the cobalt blue water.

He kicked down toward the bottom.

Was killing a wife so much different from killing a Viet Cong? He swam through the kelp forest — shimmering shafts of golden brown algae swaying with the rhythm of the surge. The leaves reminded him of nipa palms in a triple canopy jungle.

He was taken back to the time when he knew nothing about killing. He was just a young boy of nineteen on his way to a foreign country to fight a war. But, he would change forever.

It was 1967. He was stationed at Nha Be — SEAL Team headquarters in the Rung Sat Zone — Forest of Assassins. A real hell hole.

The team had been given their first mission...to wait for a VC courier, ambush him and recover intelligence. They would depart at 0100 and go northwest along the Long Tau River. They'd do an insertion in the swamp, exclusive Viet Cong real estate, and patrol the banks on foot. The area was a free fire zone — they could shoot at anything that moved.

As they geared up for the Op, Ed looked at their less than luxurious accommodations. "You ever wonder why you joined the SEALs, Mike?"

"Oh, I don't know," Mike said. "I was seventeen. I

was bored with school and skipping classes. I was hanging out at the beach and wondering what the hell I was gonna do with my life. I was going nowhere, man. Then I saw this great flick, *The Frogmen*. Adventure, heroism, the works. I walked out of that movie, thinking, 'Hey that's what I want to be – a Frogman.' One month later I faked an ID, walked down to the Navy Recruiting Office, got signed up and sworn in. They found me out two months later and sent me packing, but the minute I graduated high school I was back at it." He paused. "How about you, Ed?"

"Oh, my Dad was an Alamo Scout in World War II. I guess I wanted to be as tough as my old man."

"Yeah, well, I guess we're all out to prove ourselves in one way or another, right, buddy?"

Ed nodded.

That night they hopped in their riverine support craft, a Boston Whaler SEAL Team Assault Boat (STAB) for the expedition upriver. "Oh, shit," Mike thought, hunkering down. "This is it."

There was just a thin slit of moon. Mike and his team listened to the muffled sound of the engines as the boat made its way toward enemy territory. When they came to their insertion point, the craft slid into a mud bank bordered by mangrove trees. The roots stood out like human skeletons.

The team swam cautiously to a bank and set up an ambush position in jungle scrub. They crouched in the creaking, chirping din of the jungle with mosquitoes buzzing around their heads, but none of them dared slap the bugs for fear of warning the VC of their presence.

For the first time, Mike felt terrified. This wasn't just some training exercise at Coronado where he was trying to outsmart his instructors. He was out in the jungle, perhaps surrounded by Vietnamese, ready to shoot him!

He blinked and squeezed his eyes tight. He thought about everything but the jungle — the hug his mom gave him at the base before he left, the taste of a Budweiser at the local bar in San Diego on a Saturday night. He thought about big-breasted Marilyn Perkins, the first woman he had ever screwed.

Suddenly, he heard a mud-sucking sound along the river's edge. Squissssh. He heard it again. Squissssh. It was the sound of human feet along the riverbank.

Then, out of nowhere, the enemy appeared — a lone Vietnamese in black pajamas, no more than twenty feet from the SEALs. Mike squinted, looking around for a weapon. He didn't see one. He peered around for other Vietnamese along the riverbank. There were none.

As the squishing grew louder, he didn't think. When the enemy was ten feet away, he fired the first shot.

Instantly, the rest of the guys in his team let loose, hitting the lone Vietnamese repeatedly. When the firing was over, he followed the others out to find the VC. All that was left was blood, bone and ripped-up pajamas.

He stared at the body. Afraid he might be sick, he turned away in revulsion. He searched the brush for weapons. There were none, not even a knife. As he stood up, the underbrush at the river's edge started kicking up all around him.

"Automatic fire — ten o'clock!" the lieutenant shouted. "Get your asses down!"

Everyone dropped to the muddy ground.

Mike wildly fired off round after round from his Stoner in the direction of the shots.

"Get us outta here!" the lieutenant yelled, calling in the STAB. They raced back to the boat, escaping the fire, all except Dean Reynolds, who was wounded in the hip.

Back at the camp, Mike and the other members of his team showered while Reynolds was flown out to the hospital at Binh Thuy. Mike sat down at a wooden table in the barracks with the other guys. Bob Richter popped open several Pabst Blue Ribbons and handed them around.

Mike thought about his first kill. "I wonder why that guy didn't have a weapon."

"Maybe he wasn't a VC," Bob said. "Who knows out there in the jungle? They all look alike."

Mike suddenly put his head in his hands. It was the first time he had actually killed a person and this man might have been an innocent civilian on his way home to his family. "Oh, fuck!"

Bob threw his empty beer can down on the floor of the hootch. "Stop feeling guilty, Gallagher. They're VC, man. They aren't like you or me."

"Yeah, man, who do you want to get killed — you or a lousy VC?" Ed asked.

"I guess a lousy VC," Mike said.

Ed nodded. "You're damned right."

"No shit."

"Fucking A."

He listened to the gunfire in the distance. He lay in bed thinking of Richard Widmark swimming to the beaches in World War II. Shit, Vietnam was nothing like the movies. War wasn't about heroism and adventure. War was simply about killing.

He became hardened to the killing the day Ed Hutton died.

The war had picked up considerably. Corpses seemed to be everywhere. On their first tour, there had been minimal casualties. But they were mounting — it was only the middle of his second tour and already four of his team were dead and another two wounded. John Price lost both his legs in a land mine explosion. Henderson lost his arms in an ambush attack during a POW rescue attempt. The television and radio reported they were winning the war, but Mike had his doubts.

One night the SEALs headed downriver on the trail of some VC, supposedly traveling southeast with supplies.

Ed pulled out a pack of Camels, took one and handed another to Mike.

"So, you're gonna leave all this fun," Mike said, taking a puff and staring out into the darkness.

"You're damned right," Ed said. "I'm counting the days until I'm out of here. Me and Evelyn are getting married. I'm having a family, kids, the works, man. This jungle gives me the creeps. No targets, no visible enemies. Nothing to shoot back at. They're out there, man. Spook gooks." He shook his head. "You staying in, Shark Man?"

Mike nodded. He'd just gotten a promotion to chief. He was going to be a team leader. Anyway, he didn't care about the risk. It was worth it. He'd have several rows of medals by the time he got out and a career for life.

The next morning, the SEALs had made no headway toward locating the VC. The lieutenant decided to go into a village to question the chief.

They headed west to a village in a clearing. Bamboo thickets bordered its west flank. There were maybe a half-dozen hootches surrounded by chickens and geese pecking at the dirt. A group of old women huddled in front of one of the hootches, talking and weaving baskets.

When the SEALs arrived, the atmosphere grew quiet. A few children were chasing the chickens. One of the children ran into a hootch, and an old man with gold-framed glasses and a wispy grey beard appeared in the doorway.

The lieutenant approached the old man to talk and the SEALs relaxed a little, letting down their guard and pairing off. The SEALs weren't expecting any danger, but Mike glanced suspiciously around the village.

Suddenly, a little boy darted toward Ed.

The kid caught the SEALs' attention.

When Ed saw the boy smiling and waving, he dug in his pocket for a Hershey bar. Ed pulled the bar out of his pocket, but the kid ignored the chocolate. Instead, he ran up to Ed, reached for his belt and pulled the pin on one of his grenades. He dashed away.

Mike shouted at Ed and ducked to the ground with the other SEALs, but it was too late. Ed couldn't get the grenade unclipped. Seconds later, there was a quick dull thud as Ed's limbs were torn from him. Ed lay dead in a pool of blood.

The concussion rolled over Mike. He felt shock and then a quick heightening anger. A kid? A goddamn kid had killed Ed?

As the little boy ran away, he leveled his Stoner at the boy's shoulder blades and fired. The child's body flipped forwards in midair.

Then, wailing and crying, a woman appeared from one of the hootches and he shot her, too. There was sudden confusion in the village, Vietnamese scattering everywhere.

Mike never felt the least bit of remorse over the incident. Whether those people were civilians, whether they were women or children, whether they were friends or enemies made little difference.

Perhaps what he did that afternoon was murder. But he didn't know the difference between war and murder anymore. Did it matter if they were civilians or VC? He had a job to do and he did it. In later missions, Mike felt nothing but a rush of adrenaline when he killed.

Mike hit the ocean floor. He kicked his way through the kelp holdfasts embedded in mush and sand, toward the clifflike wall of the island. A few gobies with electric blue markings on their crimson bodies swam past him, then disappeared almost as quickly as they appeared from the cracks in the rocks.

The precipitous volcanic walls of the island were covered with algae and marine life. It was hard to locate the gap in the wall that he had found so many years ago. Finally, he spotted the yawning hole. He ventured over the threshold and entered the cave.

The cave hadn't changed. There were the same walls of grungy brown jagged rock and a light silt on the bottom. As he made his way inside, he spotted the lobsters perched along the rocky ridges.

He ventured over to the tunnel and pushed aside the silt. It rose in black clouds, muddying the water until it was murky and dim. He turned on his flashlight and peered into the long crevice.

He felt his heart quicken and the initial shock of finding the corpse resurfaced in his mind. He was surprised at his reaction. He'd seen dozens of corpses in Vietnam — corpses floating in rivers, corpses hanging from trees, corpses dismembered with their heads sticking between their legs. But, mysteriously, this body had made him uneasy, perhaps because it was the first he had seen.

Mike directed his flashlight along the bottom and the walls. There was no trace of a body.

But, he really didn't expect to find one. It would only be a skeleton by now — bits of bones tossed by the current and eaten away by salt water. Silt could have covered it up. Some sort of fish or sea animal could have found it. Or maybe, someone else had ventured into the cave, discovered it and reported it to the Coast Guard.

He looked at his dive console. He didn't have time to contemplate that corpse. He had to go ahead with his plans.

He untied the line he'd fastened to his weight belt and ran it underneath the silt, deep enough so no one would know it was there, but still shallow enough so if he dug down in the mush, he could find it. He would use that line to get out. Once he had led Cathy inside the cave, he would stir up the silt so she couldn't see, take her back into the tunnel and then jerk loose from her hand, leaving her to grope along the walls and head deep into the labyrinth. All he had to do was follow the line out of the cave, swim back to the surface and wait for Cathy to run out of air. In no time, she would drown.

His fingers trembled slightly as he finished laying the line. But as he turned back to the entranceway, he felt relieved. Calmer now, he made his way back to the chamber. His hand was steady, his swimming purposeful.

As Mike rose through the jungle of kelp, he knew he could kill Cathy.

CHAPTER

6

BUCK GRABBED HIS EMERALD windbreaker as he and Lynn
headed out the door of their house.

When they arrived at the marina, it was seven in the
morning. The marina was already bustling with activity
— fishermen heading offshore, sailboat enthusiasts unfurl-
ing their canvas and divers boarding charter boats. The
sun shone through a brilliant clear blue sky.

The *Trident* was docked not far from where they parked.
Buck recognized Mike sitting on the transom.

Mike looked eager to be off. "Morning. Ready for
some diving, guys?"

Buck nodded. "You bet. How about giving us a hand
with this gear?"

"Sure thing."

Buck handed his scuba tanks and gear to Mike who
placed them aboard at the stern. Buck loaded two large
red plastic coolers of beer and food on the boat.

"Don't forget us," said Lynn. Dressed in a natty pull-
over sweater, shorts and tennis shoes, she stepped up on

the *Trident* as Mike offered her his hand.

Lynn flashed him a glowing smile.

Mike always had too much magnetism for women, Buck thought. But he shrugged his thoughts aside, as he grabbed onto the side of the boat and jumped onboard. He took a look around the marina.

Pete Kendall, one of the playboys of Santa Barbara, had docked his sports fisher, the *Paramour*, next to the *Trident*. He had three babes on board — one blonde, one brunette and one redhead — all with gorgeous figures in itsy-bitsy bikinis under their swim cover-ups.

That was about par for Pete. He had a way with women. Buck suspected it had something to do with his gift for gab and his slim, trim body that he wrapped in skimpy trunks. His extravagant Viking 61 convertible sports fisher and the house in Hope Ranch he had inherited from his rich Dad helped, too. He often gave lavish parties. Buck suspected the babes would be topless once they were out on the water.

Buck waved at Pete. "Where're you off to?"

Pete smiled and threw a shock of dirty blond hair back from his bronzed face. "Santa Cruz Island. We're meeting Judy and Jeff Wagner for lunch. How about sharing a cold one with us?"

Buck shook his head. He knew Jeff and Judy. They were leftover hippies from the sixties.

Back then, Buck might have joined them. He had been somewhat of a hippie with a full red beard and bushy dark red hair. He'd done his share of consciousness-raising — smoked a little grass and stormed Berkeley with all the radicals protesting Vietnam. But he'd joined the Navy and his opinions changed.

"Maybe next time," Mike broke in. "We're going bug hunting."

Mike threw a hurried glance at the babes and then Pete. "Going diving?"

"So to speak." Pete grinned at the women and tossed them a boyish wink.

Buck almost laughed out loud.

"Mike's got a new cave he wants to try for bug hunting," Cathy said.

"I've dived all those caves," Pete bragged. He was also a dive instructor for NAUI. "I'd join you, but I have my hands full today." Pete glanced sideways at the blonde who was especially full breasted.

Pete waved to them as he cast off. "I'll be at Chinese Beach."

"Well, let's hope an easterly doesn't come up," Buck responded. Chinese Harbor had a small cove protected from sudden winds from the east. It had a deserted beach, perfect for Pete's plans, except when the Santa Anna winds blew in and every fisherman in the area sought shelter there.

Pete laughed. "There're no winds today. If you need anything, just give me a call."

"Okay." Buck took one last look at Pete.

Buck picked out a deck chair, grabbed some sunscreen from one of Lynn's bags, squirted the white liquid into his palm and applied it liberally to his fair skin. Later in the morning, the sun would be fierce. The smell of coconut oil hit his nostrils, followed by brewing Java.

"Coffee, anyone?" Smiling, Cathy appeared from the cabin with two steaming cups in her hand.

"Just what the doctor ordered." Buck took one of the cups for Lynn and one for himself. He looked into the salon at the small galley. A plate of uncut fruit was on the counter. A health nut, Cathy always had fruit ready about midway out. He much preferred the fruit to a large breakfast. He wasn't about to have his arteries clogged up with cholesterol.

Mike headed for the wheel at the flybridge. "We gassed up last night. A full tank."

"Great." Buck drank his coffee. "The sooner we're off, the better. It's too nice a day to wait in line at the pumps."

Mike started the engines, then maneuvered the boat out of the slip.

"So, what did you two do with the kids?" Cathy asked, turning to Lynn and Buck.

"Rosa's watching them," Lynn said.

Cathy smiled at Lynn. "I wish I had kids like yours."

"If you had to pick them up from soccer and tennis matches every day, you might change your mind," Lynn answered.

Buck stared at Lynn. She seemed to complain a lot about the boys. Didn't she even care about them?

When they were first married, all Lynn wanted was to stay home with the kids and have a house in the suburbs. But now he wasn't so sure.

"Did you see where Scott's team won the soccer championship?" Buck asked.

"Yeah, I saw that in the paper," Cathy said. "That's great, Buck."

Cathy pointed to the deck chairs. "Why don't we go sit down and let the men do the steering?"

Lynn nodded. "That's fine with me."

The two women sat down in the deck chairs in the cockpit while Buck headed for the bridge with Mike. Cathy and Lynn chatted as the boat headed out of the marina.

At the wheel, Mike reached over to the GPS, set the waypoint for Painted Cave and pushed auto. It would take a little over an hour and a half to get to the island if they continued on their present course.

It was going to be a good day. The sea was calm — great weather to cross the channel. Buck looked forward to at least two days on the boat — food prepared by Cathy, who was a premier cook, relaxation with great friends, and hopefully, a little lovemaking with Lynn.

Shrieking for some scraps, seagulls circled overhead.

Buck glanced back at the coastline. Santa Barbara was a Mediterranean mirage of red-tile roofs and thick white walls, of iron gates that led to tucked-away court- yards drenched in sunlight.

He turned back to gaze at the peaks of Santa Cruz looming in the distance. Still clouded in the brooding early morning mist, they looked faintly ominous and re- mote — ghostly wraithlike shapes floating on the ocean.

Mike nudged him. "You ever miss the Navy, Buck?"

Buck shook his head. "Nope. I can't afford to. Lynn won't let me." Navy salaries for dentists were lower than jobs on the outside.

"Well, I do," Mike said. "Excitement, fun. All the toys you could dream of — M-16s, Berettas. Life in the mud. Get shot at. Kill Charlie. That was good shit."

Getting shot at by a Chicom AK-47 wasn't Buck's idea of a good time. "I'll stick to diving," he commented.

Buck glanced at his friend. He realized how different they were. Buck would never have had the gumption to strike out on such an "iffy" venture as dive and travel.

Then again, Mike would never have the patience for dentistry. At the speciality level, root canal work required exquisite attention to detail for long hours.

For Buck, root canals were a challenge, not a chore. His files threaded the miniature canals, moving around blockages and negotiating the narrow curves that made the generalists throw in the towel.

Buck had planned his life out as exactly as if he had a map. He didn't want a lot of risks or surprises. He'd had too many as a child. All he'd ever wanted was a perfectly ordinary life — a wife, kids, a house and a job.

The time sped by. Off in the distance, he heard a rasping sound and caught sight of a telltale plume of spray from a grey whale. Mike pointed at a school of leaping porpoises about a hundred yards to starboard.

Soon the women joined them.

Cathy eased in beside Mike. "So, tell us about this new cave. My mouth is watering thinking about lobster Newburg."

Mike reached over to the autopilot and turned the knob to the right two clicks. "The cave is on the northwest side of the island, one cove west of Painted Cave. We can dive from the boat."

Cathy put her arm around Mike's waist, "What's the cave look like?"

"When you first approach it, there's an opening, perhaps twenty feet in width and height. It's sort of oval shaped, about forty-five, fifty feet wide, once inside."

"Bugs?" Cathy asked.

"They're mostly on the right side of the cave on the ledges. Hundreds of 'em. So, we'll work that side first." Mike rested his hand on the wheel. "I guarantee you won't be able to stuff your bag fast enough. All you have to do is reach out and grab 'em."

"Sounds like a tough job." Cathy winked at Buck.

Mike continued. "There's a small air pocket in the back of the cave. It's about the size of a Volkswagen cabin. We'll get to it about halfway through the dive as we work ourselves back to the left. After working the ledges, we can pop up and plan the rest of the dive."

"What's the vis like down there?" Buck asked.

"It's a little dim," Mike said. "You'd better take a light."

Buck nodded. He usually dove in open water. He rarely went in caves, but if he did, they were no more than crevices in rocks. Always the daredevil, Mike would unfasten his tank and scoot up the cracks, only taking his regulator hose with him, while Buck waited at the entranceway, ready to bag the bugs as they darted out of the cracks.

"How about taking a line?" Buck asked. He was always a detail person. He had to be organized in his work. He couldn't afford to make mistakes.

"We won't need it," Mike explained.

Buck shrugged. Although Mike could be a "macho diver" at times, he always felt safe diving with the Gallaghers, since both of them were certified NAUI instructors. Plus, he'd never seen either one of them panic in an emergency.

Buck remembered being on a group dive with the Gallaghers. One of their divers had a faulty tank. The diver had run out of air and panicked, trying to swim too quickly to the surface. Cathy had managed to offer him air from her pony tank while they both ascended slowly to the top.

Mike pointed to the far northwest side of the island. "We'll anchor in a cove near the cave. You'll get in some good sunbathing, Lynn. Anyway, there's hardly any wind."

Cathy glanced at her watch. "I don't know about you two, but I'm getting a little hungry." She got up and hurried down to the galley.

Buck hadn't realized how much time had elapsed. He could already see the craggy bluffs of Santa Cruz.

He noticed a small promontory loaded with a rookery of bull sea lions and their harem of cows. A few of the sea lions dove into the water as the *Trident* approached. The bulls were hardly bothered by the sound of the engines. One glowered over his massive shoulders and roared in true lion-like fashion.

Green was beginning to return to the landscape, replacing the desiccated brown vegetation of summer. Along the rocky coast, a couple of oystercatchers picked at clumps of washed-up kelp.

Buck looked out to sea, watching the fin of a blue interrupting the clear smooth surface. The blues were slender, graceful sharks with long pectoral fins and a great scythe of a tail. He didn't worry about blues since the larger sharks were usually in the open water, and the smaller three to four footers would avoid the divers. The same went for the nasty makos. It was the great whites that could occasionally give them some trouble.

Cathy came back up with pineapple, mangos and some bagels and handed the plate around. Buck took a few bites.

Lynn walked over to Mike at the wheel. Cathy and Buck chatted for a few moments and then joined them.

Lynn directed her attention to Buck. "Mike was telling me about his last trip to Hawaii."

"Hawaii's a great place to dive," Buck said.

"Buck has promised to take me to Hawaii," Lynn commented to Mike and Cathy. "Of course, he hasn't said when." She squared her shoulders and gave Buck a slow glare.

"Oh, Lynn, we'll get to Hawaii by June, I promise you," Buck replied, a little irritated at her prodding.

"I'll have to see it to believe it," Lynn snapped. "He's been promising since last August," she added, glancing at Cathy.

Cathy gestured with a time-out hand signal. "Okay,

you two, this is supposed to be a pleasant trip."

Mike throttled back on the powerful twin engines and maneuvered the sports fisher into a sheltered cove flanked by cliffs. They were not far from Painted Cave, probably the largest sea cave in the world.

Buck searched the horizon. No boaters were out today. The only sounds were the barks of seals, the shrieks of sea birds and the murmur of waves against the rocks and the shore.

"Okay, Buck," Mike said. "Prepare to drop anchor!"

Buck headed for the bow. He stood on the foot switch as the windlass eased the anchor to the bottom and payed out plenty of scope for a secure hold.

"Let's get into our wet suits, folks," Mike shouted. "It's time to dive!"

Cathy nodded. "Best idea we've had today."

Walking to the stern, Buck glanced at his watch — 10:30 A.M. When he reached the cockpit, he twisted it off his wrist and stuffed it in his wife's bag. None of them wore watches when they dove for bugs, for fear of scratching the crystal on the sharp rocks.

Buck looked over the equipment. Mike had brought about eight tanks — enough for several dives.

Buck grabbed one of the tanks, helped Cathy with her tank and started to gear up.

Lynn approached them. "How long will you be down?"

Mike shrugged. "About forty-five minutes."

"You won't even have time to miss us." Buck gave her a gentle pat on the hand.

She frowned. "You know I always worry when you dive, Buck."

He tried to reassure her. "You don't need to worry about us, hon. We're all experienced divers."

"I don't even know how to operate the shortwave

radio."

"You won't have to. Anyway, you have a cell phone."
Buck sighed. "Look, this is an easy dive, Lynn. If you'd
just take some lessons..."

"We've been over this before, Buck," said Lynn. "You
know I don't want to."

Buck supposed these waters could be dangerous. There
was the menace of ever-present sharks and the surges
could get fierce, tossing divers around like a tornado.

But the Channel Islands were the only real place to
dive off Santa Barbara. Plenty of people came here on
the weekends, although most of them went to the south
side of the island which was protected from the winds.

Buck nodded to Lynn. "You think about a great lobster
dinner. We'll be back in no time." He gave her a quick
kiss.

"I guess I'll start on my suntan." She resigned herself
to one of the deck chairs and grabbed her sunglasses
from the table.

Buck took one last look at his wife, wrapped in a
turquoise bikini which showed off her deep tan. She
propped herself up in the chair and began rubbing suntan
oil on her long limbs. With her trim waist and ample
breasts, she looked remarkably good for her forty-one
years.

Buck had seen the looks men gave Lynn when they
went out together. He'd even seen Mike give her a few
glances. She was one very sexy woman.

"Hey, Buck, are you ready?" Cathy yelled from the
dive ladder.

"Yeah, I'm ready." Buck turned away from his wife.

He hooked a flashlight to his buoyancy compensator
(BC) and finished gearing up. Reflecting off his wet suit,
the sun felt warm.

"Okay guys, let's go!" shouted Mike as he jumped fins first into the water, followed by Cathy.

The conversation with Lynn was all but forgotten. Buck was looking forward to lavender gorgonians and bright orange garibaldi and leafy golden kelp forests.

Buck let out a whoop. "All right! Let's bag some bugs!" Seconds later, his body hit the chilled water.

CHAPTER

7

Lynn watched the three divers disappear beneath the surface.

The water was becoming choppier. The wind and current created little whitecaps on the ocean's surface. The tide was coming in.

From the north, a sudden wind blew strands of her dark hair across her face. She put down her book, pulled a scarf out of her beach bag and tied her hair back.

She knew she should have stayed at home. Years ago, she hadn't minded; but now, with the affair, it was awkward coming on these trips with the Gallaghers. She didn't like being around Cathy when she was with Mike.

Plus, she wondered how long she could hide her reactions to Mike. She'd felt Buck's eyes on her during the whole trip to Santa Cruz Island. Suppose he suspected. He could throw her out of the house. She'd lose everything — the house, the kids, her social status. She felt terrified at that thought.

She turned her mind to other things — the glances

Mike had given her coming over on the boat, her previous conversation with Mike in the hotel room and his last kiss. When Mike kissed her, his warmth flowed right through her body, and all her qualms disappeared.

If she thought about it deeply enough, she could almost feel the roughness of stubble on his chin. He smelled faintly of lemon lime aftershave. She loved that smell. She'd never been able to resist Mike.

He had a sort of animal magnetism and enthusiasm that Buck lacked. He made her feel like no man had ever existed before him.

He reminded her of someone, perhaps her father, a pilot in the Air Force — a dashing, handsome man with brown hair and deep blue eyes. She was his favorite of three children. Sometimes, he'd take her up in a plane and they'd soar over the mountains and ocean.

But he'd died when she was nine. She had never gotten over his death.

She sighed, brushed back a strand of dark hair with her fingertips, reached for her bag on her chair, and grabbed a pack of Virginia slims and a gold lighter. She lit a cigarette, took a deep breath and exhaled slowly, feeling a sense of freedom. It wasn't often she had a chance to smoke. Buck had sinus problems and he wouldn't allow it.

She supposed she was enthralled with Mike — his celebrity, his travel and his wealth. He certainly wasn't like Buck's other friends — specialists in the medical profession who bored her to tears with shop talk.

"God, I wish I'd never had an affair with you," she had told Mike once. She hadn't realized how unhappy she was with Buck until that moment.

"You don't mean that and you know it. "

He was right. "Well, I never cheated on Buck until I

met you," she said.

"There's a first time for everything, Lynn," he had an-swered, kissing her and she had melted into his arms.

Mike made her want to walk away from her marriage instantly, but she didn't have the means. She didn't want to go back to the life she had lived as a child.

When her father had died, her family could barely cover expenses, even with the GI insurance. Her mother was soon forced to take secretarial jobs, working long hours just to make ends meet.

"You find a man and hold onto him," her mother had told her. "Don't end up like me. "

Often, she had to wear hand-me-downs from her older sisters. The other children in her neighborhood called her "Raggedy Ann. "

She thought things would be different when she mar-ried Buck. She was impressed with him. He was worldly, sophisticated, spoke several languages and had plans to be a doctor. She assumed he could give her what she lacked in life.

But shortly after they were married, she realized she'd made a mistake. Buck joined the Navy, explaining it was a way to support them and get assistance with medical school.

She was horrified. She didn't want a military man for a husband. Plus, his salary wasn't that high. She was still in college herself and had to work while attending school.

She began to have nightmares of ending up destitute like her mother.

She thought about leaving him then. She actually packed her bags and went down to the bus station one day, but then realized she had no place to go. So, she went home.

She just held on, knowing it was only a short while

until Buck became a doctor. But when his time was up, Buck opted out of medical school to become a dentist. She was extremely disappointed. Yet, she rationalized she'd come this far with him, so she stayed.

When Kevin was born and Buck finished dental school, he opened his practice and she quit her menial teaching job. She went out of her way to socialize in order to build Buck's clientele.

Then, finally, after years of struggle, she had a house in Hope Ranch, kids, new cars, designer clothes and a husband who was part of the medical community.

But just when she thought all Buck's promises were coming true, they had financial problems. In the last several years, Buck made a series of bad investments. He put a damper on her spending. He threatened to pull Scott out of private school. He argued about her buying a new car. He was planning on dropping their membership in the La Cumbre Country Club. Suppose she could no longer play tennis at the club. She'd lose a lot of her friends.

She felt cheated. After all, she had raised his children, done all the housework, and put her time and energy into boosting his career and moving him up the social ladder.

After Kevin, she vowed she would have no more children. She didn't want to get like Buck's mother, a devout Catholic, who popped out kids like a toaster oven. Lynn had almost lost her figure with Kevin.

Two years ago, she gave Buck an ultimatum. No more kids. She had her tubes tied. Buck had put up a bitter fight. But she won out. She was out of the baby-making business.

After she met Mike, she thought she had a chance at happiness. He was everything Buck wasn't — exciting, rich. She could walk away from Buck in a heartbeat. But if she left the kids with Buck, she wouldn't get a penny.

She had thought eventually Mike would divorce Cathy and marry her, but she hadn't known about his financial situation until that day in the hotel room. Now, she had to contend with Cathy. Her eyes narrowed.

She lit a second cigarette. Her eyes drifted again to the ocean. She blew smoke rings into the air, finished the cigarette, then tossed it over the rail. She looked at her watch. Two minutes had passed. She picked up the book.

Lynn remembered Mike's words in the hotel room, "Now you didn't mean that, did you, Lynn?" he'd asked. No, she did mean it, she thought. Perhaps it was awful, but she didn't care. She did wish Cathy were dead.

After Buck jumped into the chilled water, he had shut his eyes momentarily.

Now, opening them, he found himself suspended and near weightless in another universe — serene and beautiful.

The cold water began filtering through his suit and his gloves. Then it warmed, held by the close-fitting rubber.

Turning himself toward the island wall, he paused for a moment to get his bearings. He spotted Cathy's bright orange game bag just ahead. He let air out of his BC and descended with the Gallaghers into the kelp forest — a mass of swaying vegetation.

The kelp leaves reminded him of ancient Chinese matted prints, paper-thin and golden brown. Shimmering shafts of light streaked through the blades of kelp, gently following the rhythm of the surge. Sunlight bounced off the leaves, transforming the water into a sea of amber with clear blue patches.

But as he descended, visibility dimmed. He swallowed and worked his jaw. His ears cleared with a fizzing snap, and he blew a little air into his BC until he was neutral.

Once the divers hit bottom, they swam toward the abrupt vertical escarpment of the wall — dark brown rock made from marine sediment deposits and volcanic eruptions, sprinkled with a unique ecosystem of underwater life — orange cup corals, blood stars, encrusting sponges, California golden gorgonians, feathery crinoids, flowerlike hydroids, ghostly white plumrose anemones and scallops.

This was a macrophotographer's heaven! Buck would have liked to linger and do some sight-seeing or take pictures, but he didn't want to lose Mike and Cathy. They were moving quickly toward a deep crevice in the wall.

He happened to glance at his dive console as they approached the cave. They had descended about twenty-five feet — a shallow dive.

Just up ahead was a large black gaping hole on the west wall of the cove. He saw Cathy and Mike disappear into the yawning archway. He followed them inside.

Wow! Buck had seen only small caves. This thing was mammoth! His heartbeat quickened in anticipation.

It wasn't completely dark inside the chamber; the dimmed light gave it a twilight effect. Beams of light streamed through the aperture of the cave. There was no need for a flashlight.

He followed Mike and Cathy along the right side of the wall. The cave was made of chunky brown rock filled with stair-stepping ledges and rocky crevices.

Almost immediately, he saw the familiar brick red color of a five-pound lobster perched on a crevice just in front of him. With its hard exoskeleton and long front antennae, the bug looked like an ancient armored knight wielding two piercing lances, ready to do battle.

Buck's eyes adjusted to the darkness. He moved in closer. At least six more lobsters were perched on the ledges of the wall in the back of the cave. This was going to be easier than standing in line at the Santa Barbara Shellfish Company.

Mike was already pouncing on his prey, a gigantic bug, maybe fifteen pounds.

Buck turned his attention to the task at hand — bagging his own bugs for dinner. Scouring the rock for a tasty crustacean, he moved in closer to the wall and shone his flashlight up the rock. Not more than five feet from him, he sighted an eight-pounder. Buck rested his light on a nearby ledge. Then, the lobster immediately oriented itself toward the beam of light.

Buck swam to the other side and floated up a little higher until he was hovering over the creature. Careful not to give himself away, he moved in slowly. The lobster's antennae were exquisitely sensitive to small disturbances in the water and he wanted to avoid spooking it.

Exhaling slowly, he drifted down until he was about arm's reach from the creature. He was careful to avoid the sharp spines along the perimeter of the tail where he could lose his grip.

Lunging for a spot between the tail and the carapace, Buck made his move. As he grasped the body, he felt a strong tail flick, then a powerful yank as the lobster struggled to get away.

He wrestled with the creature. Finally managing to subdue it, he undid his game bag snap and pushed the lobster inside, tail first. Once the bug was bagged, he snapped the top shut. He heard the clicking of the wriggling body as it struggled to escape.

He began to work himself up one side of the wall, bagging another lobster and then another. The clicking noises became more audible as the bagged lobsters flopped against each other.

Buck felt a rush of adrenaline. This was fun! It was a challenge to see if he could outsmart the bugs. Sometimes he missed one, but more often than not, he bagged the wily critters. This was one of the best dives he had been on with Mike.

He worked himself about halfway up from the sandy bottom to the ceiling, and bagged another lobster along the way. He figured he'd covered maybe ten or eleven feet. The cave really wasn't that high.

But he suddenly realized it was getting darker. He peered around. Odd, he thought. Visibility was not all that good. Actually, it was downright lousy.

What had happened? The cave was silting up. Dark cloudlike layers of dust drifted in the water. He'd been so busy trying to get the lobsters, he hadn't realized how much silt he and the other divers had kicked up. Now it engulfed him like L. A. smog.

He groped blindly and fought off the urge to panic. He was in an unknown cave with a limited amount of air, and Mike and Cathy were nowhere in sight.

He tipped his head forward to rinse his mask, but visibility was still terrible. He felt his heart tripping against his rib cage. Okay, Buck, the fun's over, he thought. It's time to get the hell out.

Instinctively, he dropped to the bottom. But visibility became so bad he couldn't see more than six inches in front of him. He reached down by his knees and felt soft gushy mud — the source of all the silt.

He remembered his wife's words, "What if something goes wrong?" Well, nothing had gone wrong. He just needed to find Mike and Cathy and get back to the boat.

He suddenly felt a fin, either Mike or Cathy. He worked his way up the leg, groping at the knee. A hand grasped his. It was Cathy. She stopped. He suspected Mike was just up ahead of her.

Buck moved up to Cathy's face mask. She was hand signaling to him — pointing upwards and shining her flashlight at the surface.

Directly overhead, he could make out the shape of a small air chamber. It shone like mercury — a silvery interface between water and air.

Obviously, Cathy wanted to surface and talk.

He nodded and waited while she turned away. He suspected she was getting Mike.

Then she took his hand and led him up. He and Cathy hit the surface in a matter of seconds, followed by Mike.

The chamber was small. They were only a few inches from each other. It was tight quarters.

Buck jerked the regulator out of his mouth and took a gulp of air. He grimaced. The air was musty, stale. He shoved his mask up. "I can't see a thing with all this shit. What do you say we call this a day?"

"I'm with Buck," Cathy agreed. "We've got our bugs. Let's get back to the boat and have some lunch. I'd like to catch a few rays."

"That's fine," Mike said. "I'll take the lead. You guys grab onto each other and me. We'll work our way around on the left back to the entrance, okay?"

Buck nodded. "Sounds good to me. How long have we been down, anyway?"

Mike looked at his console. "I don't know, maybe fifteen minutes."

"Well, let's go, guys," said Cathy firmly. "Or, would you two men like to continue your little morning chat?"

"*Moi?*" Buck pointed to his mask and looked guiltily at Mike.

Cathy nodded and frowned. "*Oui, Monsieur Connors, vous.* Who else, may I ask, is down here?"

Buck panned a beam of light around the cave.

Mike laughed.

Cathy rolled her eyes.

The three of them repositioned their gear and then sank once more into the murky water.

Mike led; Cathy followed; and Buck brought up the rear.

They all went down to the bottom again. The bottom was pure mush. Buck sucked mud like a snail, tasting the sulfurous seepage through his mouthpiece.

As they moved, Cathy and Mike's flippers stirred up more silt. Buck couldn't see diddly-squat. Silt was every-where — in his hair, on Cathy's flippers, even between his gloves. If he hadn't had on a regulator, he would have breathed the damned stuff.

Buck was following close behind Cathy when she abruptly stopped. What was she doing? Turning around? She came mask-to-mask with him.

He purged a spoonful of murky water from his mask. Then he switched on his flashlight. He shone the beam directly under her face. Cathy was hand signaling again, wildly shaking her head back and forth and waving her hands in dismay.

Uh, ohh, he thought. She'd lost Mike. She'd probably lost her grip on him. He felt a little irritated at Cathy for turning around and not continuing in the same direction. Why hadn't she just kept going? She would have bumped into Mike again.

He said a few prayers to the Great Blue Gods of the Deep. Probably Mike was just up ahead, waiting for them.

He motioned for Cathy to grab his weight belt, and this time, he took the lead. He knew the configuration of the cave. The entrance was located only thirty feet away. It was logical if they worked their way back across the cave, they'd get out. That was a scientific fact and Buck was a great believer in science.

He started out again, keeping his fins up and his head down, doing a cautious shuffle kick to avoid stirring up the silt, but it wasn't that easy. The Great Blue Gods had not answered his prayers.

He made his way hand over hand along the wall, as his knees dragged through the mud. It was useless turning on the flashlight. It was like turning on the brights of a car in dense fog. Still, he didn't feel as if he had to have a flashlight. He'd done a lot of night diving. He tried to cover as much ground as possible without stirring up the silt.

Suddenly, he felt a tug at his weight belt. He stopped for a moment and went face-to-face with Cathy. He turned on the flashlight. She was pointing to her instruments and gauges. He peered closer, focusing on her wrist.

The needle on her compass was pointing north. The entrance of the cave faced northeast. But they were going south. He hadn't changed directions. What the fuck was going on? He glanced at Cathy again. Her eyes were wide; she seemed confused.

He took a look at his dive console. The luminescent numbers told him he had to hustle. They didn't have much air. He gave Cathy a reassuring squeeze on the shoulder and swam.

He decided to go up to the top of the cave again where visibility was better, but he banged his head on some rock. Ouch! The ceiling had peaked out. He couldn't remember the ceiling ever being that low.

He went to the bottom and progressed a little farther. There was another thump on his head as his face mask crunched into more rock. He thrust his arms forward and touched rock on all three sides. Where the hell were they?

He paused, trying to get his bearing. This didn't make sense... unless.... Maybe the silt had covered up another tunnel in the cave. That was the only explanation. The cave must have extended farther back than Mike had thought. They must be on some alternate geologic fault line intersecting with the main fault. Mike had given them the wrong configuration.

He felt an overwhelming sickening sensation. They were in some sort of constricted passageway. There was nothing to do but back away, turn around and retrace their steps.

They did a 180 and started out again.

Cathy pushed him so he would move faster. But in a few minutes, he hit another dead end. He had the impression he was going around in circles. He gritted his teeth in frustration. Being slam dunked into rock wasn't his idea of fun. Mike should have checked out this cave.

By the way, where the hell was Mike?

Exasperated, Buck realized they were lost. He'd bounced into so many spots, it was hard to tell whether he'd been there before or not.

He took a look at his pressure gauge. He had only 1,500 PSI — about thirty minutes of air. He stopped for a moment, silently reflecting on his situation. It definitely was getting worse.

Kaboom. Kaboom. Was that his heart? It was probably pumping a good 120. He was taking in huge breaths from his regulator.

He quickly forced himself to stop gulping in air. He concentrated on doing a couple of breathing exercises. The regulator hose was his lifeline to a limited supply of air and it was running lower with each passing second.

Cathy yanked at his belt. She was right. They couldn't

stay in one place; they had to haul some ass.

But the problem was, he didn't know where to go. They were trapped. They were lost deep in the claws of a twisted black labyrinth — and Buck finally had to face the possibility that they might not find their way out.

CHAPTER

8

IT WAS THE PERFECT murder. A couple of divers go out to do some bug hunting. No one takes a line. The cave gets silted up. The divers lose their way. They run out of air and drown.

Mike could already see the headline in the *News-Press.* "Tragic Diving Accident Claims Lives — Drowning At Santa Cruz Island." The paper would probably carry Cathy's picture below the headline — Cathy with a smile on her face and a gleam in her eye; not the Cathy they would pull from the cave, her face white, her hair matted with kelp, her lips blue — Cathy, a corpse.

The paper would also carry a photo of Buck — maybe one from the Navy. It would be beside Cathy's. Buck with a grin on his face, his hair in a crew cut, a white officer's hat on his head.

Mike didn't like the idea of killing Buck, but there wasn't much he could do about him coming along on the trip, especially since Cathy had extended the open invitation. He had to go ahead with his plans. He might not get another chance, especially once Cathy found out he was lying about that contract. He also didn't want her to sell the business.

Mike wasn't completely hardened to the deaths. He regretted having to kill his wife and his friend, but not enough to stop this murder.

Memories came back of earlier times with Cathy — small things — the touch of her hand against his shoulder, the flash of her blonde hair in the sunlight, the sound of her laughter. He remembered the way she looked yesterday afternoon as she cleaned the deck — a look of anticipation on her face, flashing constant smiles, as if she really thought that things might work out between them.

But he knew their marriage would never work out. What he was doing now was simply a matter of survival. Any emotions he had were not his own, as if they were in some other body, somewhere else.

He dug down in the mud. Perhaps he had just buried his emotions the way he had buried the line. He felt the line between his fingers and began to move forward, slowly swimming toward the mouth of the tunnel.

As he swam farther and farther away from the two divers, he went over his plans in his mind. He knew how important it was to make this look like an accident. So, as soon as he got back to the boat, he planned to fake a small rescue attempt.

He'd run another line into the cave, and in addition, take some extra tanks and bleed them to make it look like he was searching for the divers. He'd stay awhile, just long enough to make sure the two divers were dead, then he'd surface, go back to the boat and radio the Coast Guard. The Coast Guard would probably radio the Ventura County Sheriff's Department and the National Park Service ranger at Scorpion Canyon to send out a search and rescue team.

He'd been on a few dives with the team and he knew how long they would take to get to Santa Cruz Island. They'd have to call up volunteers, ready up a crew and get their gear together. Then they'd have to locate a boat, get the crew on board, and make their way out to the island to find the *Trident*.

By his best guesstimate, it would take three and a half-hours. The two would be dead long before the Coast Guard arrived — victims of this labyrinth.

It was the perfect murder — almost. There was a small problem. The officers would ask why he hadn't taken a line.

As a NAUI instructor, he'd been trained to take lines into caves or wrecks. It was standard procedure, although there were plenty of experienced divers who didn't follow procedure, especially when caves were easy, shallow and without tunnels.

That was his excuse. The cave looked easy. With the silt covering the entrance to the tunnel, it seemed like an uncomplicated dive. There was no need for a line.

It was fortunate that Lynn was along, even though he hadn't counted on her being there at first. She could be his alibi. She could corroborate his story — that this was just an innocent dive trip, that they had all gone down to catch lobsters, and Buck and Cathy had gotten lost.

He was sure Cathy's father would raise some questions. After all, Cathy was his only daughter and he had never liked Mike. Still, they couldn't arrest him just on her father's suspicions.

He suspected the sheriff's department would take him down to the station for questioning. He'd been down to that station once on a traffic accident, and he'd seen the interrogation room. Sterile. White. There would probably be two officers. They'd start out easy with him, be polite, offer him a cup of coffee. They'd ask him to go over all the details.

Then they'd start asking the really important questions. Like if there was any trouble in the marriage. Any stress. They'd ask him if there were any recent arguments. He'd deny it all, of course. No one knew about their arguments.

The officers would probably do some investigating into the finances. Find out the dive business wasn't doing well. But the business had been going downhill for years. Again, there was nothing they could prove.

They might even ask him about his time spent in Vietnam. His background. "Didn't kill no kids, no women," they'd ask.

"No," he would say. "Nothing like that."

That would be a lie, but there was no evidence to convict him. The SEALs had never reported the incident.

The way he figured it, the officers could try, but they would have a hard time proving he was a killer. Most likely, they would report his wife's murder as an accident, even if they did investigate.

Mike was sure he wouldn't get caught. Any regrets he might have from Cathy's death were overpowered by thoughts of his future. The threats and arguments with Cathy would be over now, part of his past.

Yet as he swam away from the scene of his crime, he began to have some doubts. He thought of other possibilities. His mind returned to Ed Hutton.

As far as Mike knew, the secret of the cave had died the day Hutton was killed. But maybe his buddy had broken his vow of silence. What if some witness appeared out of nowhere, verifying Ed's story about the cave and the body?

As Mike made his way forward, his light probing the obsidian blackness of the narrow tunnel, the doubts grew stronger. He felt uneasy. He glanced at his dive console.

It hit him full force that in twenty minutes his wife and one of his best buddies would be dead, and he was the culprit. He had cold-bloodedly plotted their deaths. No jury would let him off.

Suppose he was convicted of murder? Suppose he had to live the rest of his life in a cold dark jail cell?

The possibility of a prison term loomed before him, terrifying and hideous.

He felt his heart pounding with dread.

In a moment of fear, or perhaps panic, he back-kicked and turned around, starting back in the direction from where he had come, searching for Buck and Cathy. But the silt had cut visibility to only six inches, and as he groped the water for a flipper, a mask, a limb, there was only open space.

Abruptly, he stopped, questioning his actions. He realized Cathy and Buck could be anywhere in the maze by now. He'd never find them in the next half-hour and that was all the air he had left.

To make matters worse, he'd used up ten minutes of precious air in this rescue attempt — air he didn't have to waste. He'd been a fool! Had he forgotten everything he'd learned in SEAL training? If there was one thing his instructor had taught him, it was never to hesitate. Hesitation could cost a life — his own.

Hesitation was a sign of emotional conflict and he'd let his emotions get in the way. In a moment of panic, he'd made a mistake.

Even if someone came forward and testified against him, it was all hearsay. There was no proof of his guilt.

He clenched his fists together in fury. Oh, shit! There

was nothing between them. He realized in his panic to find the two divers, he had gone off searching in another direction and let go of his line.

In terror, he turned around in the opposite direction and started back toward the main chamber. Only, he couldn't be sure he was headed in the right direction. For all he knew, he could be heading deeper and deeper into the labyrinth.

What if he was in some unknown tunnel? He was as good as dead.

He felt his heart skip a beat.

He glanced at his wrist, trying to gain some reassurance from his instruments, but realized that his compass was of no use at all in this maze. Fingerlike side channels splayed off in all directions. He could be headed down a finger toward a dead end.

He started hyperventilating, gasping mouthfuls of dry metallic tasting air. The bubbles sizzled from his tank. His heart pounded against his rib cage. Was he panicking? That was the worst thing he could possibly do.

He took a moment and tried his best to calm down. He did his breathing exercises. That felt better. The air bubbles slowed to a steady upward stream.

He stopped in his pathway and rethought his situation. Slowly valving a little air out of his BC, he descended to the bottom again. He dug down into the muck, burying his gloves in the debris.

Go easy, Mikey boy. Look for the line. If he didn't find that line, he'd die here in this watery grave, his own killer. How stupid could he get? It was worse than tripping over one of his own booby traps in the Mekong Delta. He had to find that line.

He dug down and clumsily grappled along the bottom, his fingers like blind anemones. He felt along the wall, but his fingertips found only rock and silt.

He swam forward, knocking his head against one of the rocks. A cascade of rubble tumbled over his head and chest.

Damn! His head and back throbbed with pain. He was gulping his air. He paused. Get your thoughts together, Mikey boy. Look for the line.

He took a deep breath of air and blew it out slowly...thinking. He was certain he had laid the line just beneath him. What had changed? Nothing but the piling up of more light sediment. Hell, he knew where the line was located.

Pushing aside more muck, he dug deeper. Eureka! He felt the reassuring cord between his gloves. He grasped it and tugged, letting his fingers do the walking through the watery morass toward the entrance to the cave.

Hand over hand. He was practically crawling through the water and all he could see was darkness and hard, jagged rock.

He finally saw a dim circle of grey in the distance — evidence of the tunnel's entrance. He shoved on, over rocks and through mud. Another twenty feet and he had made it. Home safe.

He felt a flood of relief, as if he had returned from the grave. He followed the line around the walls of the chamber until he finally was in open water. He shook himself free from all that silt and debris, and any remorse he might have felt at Cathy and Buck's death.

He followed the line to an overhanging rock outside the cave that was surrounded by kelp where he had tied the rope. He untied it and placed it in his dive bag. Then he swam toward the boat.

Cathy and Buck were probably panicking at this moment, kicking up more silt and using up their precious supply of air. He, on the other hand, was calm.

He swam upward through the kelp jungle into the world of light. The cold blue underwater world regained its colorful spectrum of warm vibrant reds, oranges and yellows. He broke the surface in a matter of minutes.

Overhead, sea gulls shrieked. In the distance, he heard the barking of harbor seals. Waves lapped calmly against the bow of the *Trident*. He wasn't far from the boat.

Lynn stood at the cockpit, her hands shading her eyes as she scanned the sea.

He noticed the water was becoming rougher. He swam closer to the boat and pulled himself up onto the dive ladder.

"Where're Cathy and Buck?" Lynn asked. She helped him out of his gear.

"In the cave," he said. He took off his tank and fins, then walked across the deck. "I lost them."

"Lost them!" Her eyebrows rose in surprise. "How could you...?"

"There are a lot of mazes in that cave. They're in a tunnel somewhere."

"Well, what are you going to do?"

Mike grinned. "I thought I'd leave them there."

Lynn's mouth opened in amazement. "But they'll be killed!"

"That's the idea." He unzipped his wet suit.

"But..." she began.

He interrupted. "Look, Lynn, this was all your idea."

"What are you talking about?"

"You said you wished Cathy was dead."

She gasped. "Yes, but I never thought you'd do this..."

He grabbed a towel to dry off. "Well, it seemed the only way."

She shook her head.

"Anyway, there was no time. She was planning on selling my business. She wanted a separation. I would have gotten no money. It was either now or never."

She gritted her teeth. "And Buck, what about Buck?"

He threw the towel on the deck. "I thought you said you didn't have any feelings for Buck."

"I said I didn't love him. That doesn't mean I want him dead."

He took her hand and squeezed it.

She jerked her hand away. "God, I can't believe you actually did this!"

"Don't tell me you're having doubts. It's a little late."

She put her head in her hands. "This is too complicated."

"Look, Lynn, they would have found out about the affair. Buck would have divorced you. You couldn't have a house in Hope Ranch on his child support."

Guiltily, she looked at the deck. She frowned. "I don't like this, not at all," she protested.

"Ah, c'mon, Lynn. I did it all for you, babe." He grabbed her by the waist, pulled her to him and kissed her deeply.

She pulled away from his grasp.

"What if the police suspect me?" she asked.

"Look, Lynn, you've been on deck the whole time. You're an innocent bystander."

"They could find out about us."

"They're not going to find out." He paused. "Just stop worrying. I'll run a line down and use up all the extra tanks of air. They'll assume it was an accident and I tried to find them. Just relax."

"What time is it?"

"Noon."

"Suppose Buck and Cathy find their way out?" She

turned around to face him and eased closer.

"It's impossible. By my calculations, they're already dead. They only had forty-five minutes of air. Their time's already up. Just relax, babe," he said, smiling. "In a couple of minutes, I'll put in a call to the Coast Guard. Make it look real. Believe me. Nothing, absolutely nothing, is gonna go wrong."

CHAPTER

9

BOOM! BOOM! BUCK'S HEART pounded so loudly he thought the walls of the cave were vibrating.

Although he tried to control his initial panic, he was feeling claustrophobic. He didn't know where in the hell he was, and even with the flashlight, he couldn't see more than a few inches in front of him. Plus, his air was running lower and lower with every second.

In a normal situation, twenty-five feet below the surface, when things got bad, he could have bailed out. Just dumped his weight belt, inflated his BC vest and floated back to the surface. But right above him was solid rock, a good ten million years of it — centuries of lava flows and marine fossils weighing down on his shoulders. If he tried to surface, he'd slam right into it.

He listened, straining to hear anything from the surface — a roar of a motor, the barking of seals. Then, he might know which way to go. But there was no sound, only the steady thump of his heartbeat, the click and hiss of the regulator as he inhaled, and the muffled roar of air bubbles rising from his tank.

Hesitating, he hovered motionless in the constricted passageway while the silence swelled, grew enormous around the helpless pulse of his heartbeat. He was engulfed by the eternal, absolute blackness of the cave.

Impatiently, Cathy tugged on Buck's weight belt. She was right. They had to go somewhere. But where?

Buck turned around, dragging Cathy along like a puppy dog on a chain through the silty mud. He bore onward, but banged his head on the jagged rock that jutted out from the walls of the cave.

He finned forward, a little more carefully, and luckily, this time, he didn't reach a dead end. Thank God! He began to feel a little better. Maybe they were headed in the right direction.

He moved up a little higher where the water was clearer. Suddenly, he felt less resistance in the water. He broke the surface. He heard a splash as Cathy surfaced after him.

He switched on his dive light. The beam dissipated in foggy droplets of moisture. It flickered over jutting rocks and craggy notches of broken fossils embedded in porous dark brown rock.

They'd hit some sort of air pocket, similar to the one earlier in the main chamber. The room looked huge in the thin beam of his flashlight. It was shaped like a pyramid — higher in the center, elongated at both ends and feathering off at the sides. It was about ten or twelve feet high and eight feet wide, probably formed from incoming ocean swells.

He flipped up his mask and took the regulator out of his mouth. The stale air was heavy with moisture. He coughed and cleared his throat.

"Thank God, we've found some air!" Cathy exclaimed.

"Every time I looked at my regulator getting lower and lower, my heart started beating like crazy."

"Yeah, mine too." Buck's heart slowed down. For the moment, they were in a better situation. At least he could see and even though the air was noxious, he could breathe. He felt his initial anxiety dissipating, blowing off as he breathed without the aid of his tanks.

Cathy removed her mask. "Where are we?"

"I don't know. But at least we've got air." Buck jerked his head around. "Where the hell is Mike?"

Her eyes opened wide. "One minute I was holding him, and the next minute he was gone. I can't figure it out. He probably turned quickly. My hand was knocked loose." She shrugged.

"Christ," he muttered. "How much air do you think we have in here?" he asked.

"Maybe a couple of hours. If we were near the surface, I'd say there might be an opening to the outside and it would be unlimited."

"Do you hear any sea lions barking?" He thought his ears might be clogged with water.

She shook her head. "I don't hear anything."

"That means we're probably down pretty deep, and the air's limited. What do you think we should do?"

"I don't know. But we need to stay calm. The more we panic, the more air we use up."

"Yeah, I know." Buck sneezed. His allergies were bothering him. He wished he'd taken a Seldane before the dive.

The water level rose slightly. Immediately, the air compressed and condensed the moisture into a super thick fog, dense and white. He began to get a sinus squeeze. "Cathy, I'm going to turn off the dive light. There's no telling how much longer the batteries will last."

"Okay."

He shut off the light. It was pitch black. Spooky. He turned the light back on and scratched his chin. How were they going to get out of this place?

He brooded for a while longer. Finally, he spoke. "We've got to get out of here."

"Look, Mike's probably made it to safety," Cathy said with feigned cheerfulness. "He'll come rescue us."

Buck sighed. Cathy was always such an optimist. No one was going to come and rescue them. No one had the slightest idea where they were.

He felt anxious. "I'm going to head out in that direction." He pointed the flashlight beam to the corner of the cave from where they had come. "Are you ready to try again?"

"Yeah."

"Hold onto my weight belt. Don't let go, no matter what, okay?"

She nodded.

He turned off the light and strapped it down. He adjusted his mask, put his regulator in his mouth and slipped down into the water again. Cathy held onto his weight belt. He moved briskly, but visibility was still poor.

He worked himself around the wall, but it ended in a cul-de-sac. Shit! No exit. He felt like he was entering a glove with fingers branching off in every direction. He worked his way back up and got some more space.

The tunnel finally opened up again; it wasn't so narrow. All right! Yes! They were heading out of the tunnel, he just knew it! He swam maybe another five feet and felt a sense of buoyancy. He broke the surface with a splash.

He reached for his flashlight, switched it on and shone the beam upwards.

"Oh, damn!" he said disappointed. He immediately

recognized the familiar shape of the original cavern. They were back where they'd started.

He glanced at Cathy's crestfallen face.

"We're going around in circles!" she said.

"I know." Getting out of this hellhole was going to be really tough.

"I'm getting cramps in my legs," she complained, treading water. "I want to sit down."

"That makes two of us." Buck shone his light around the cavern, but there was only rough, jagged sharp rock — no fish or crabs or barnacles or algae. Nothing at all living. Just the darkness and the rock and the fog. He spotted a small ledge in the corner just large enough for two people.

"Let's get out of our gear," Buck said. "Then we can sit down." He pointed to the ledge with his flashlight.

"Good idea." Cathy half swam, half waded through the oozy sticky mud to the ledge.

Sloshing through the water, he followed in her finsteps. They both undid their weight belts and propped them up on the ledge, then slipped out of their BC vests, inflated them and left them floating on the surface of the water.

They hopped up on the rocky seat. The sharp jagged rock dug into his back.

He sneezed again. He realized his sneezing coincided with the normal swell cycle. With every incoming surge, the water level rose an inch or two, and, in turn, the pressure rose, creating a thick fog. It made breathing difficult. Then, as the surge retreated, the water subsided and the pressure returned to normal again.

Cathy sighed. "Buck, are we going to die in this place?"

He hadn't expected that from Cathy. She was always

Miss Pollyanna Positive. "Of course not."

"What if there's no way out?"

"There's a way out. There was a way in, wasn't there?"

"Yeah, I guess so. That makes sense."

He paused. "Look, I've been in a lot of tight spots in my life. I've always gotten out."

"Like when?"

He couldn't think of one tight spot he'd been in. "Oh, when I was trying to date two girls at the same time. That's a hell of a tight spot."

She burst into laughter and the muffled sound echoed off the walls of the cave. It was eerie, as if other voices were mocking them, but there was no one else in the cave.

Then Cathy's tone grew serious. "Suppose Mike didn't make it out either. Suppose he's in one of these tunnels like us."

"Naw, Jeez, he was a Navy SEAL."

"I know, I know," she said. "Navy SEALs never say die."

He felt a sudden sharp prick in his spine. The rocks felt like daggers. "I feel like floating, Cathy. My back's killing me."

He plopped into the water, retrieved his BC and climbed into his vest. The water was chilly, but at least he didn't have those rocks sticking into his back.

Cathy's voice quivered. "You know, all I can think about is Mike, wondering if he's okay."

He nudged her with his toe. "Mike's a survivor. He'll get out."

"I guess so." She rubbed her wrist. "Jesus, my wrist hurts."

"Why?"

Cathy frowned. "Something hit my wrist just before I

lost my grip on Mike." Cathy turned her wrist over in the palm of her other hand.

Buck shook his head, angry at Mike. "Damn! How could Mike lose us? Why didn't he grab you again?"

"Well, you know, Mike has problems with vertigo. He ruptured his eardrum in a dive off Australia's Great Barrier Reef last year. He could have lost his equilibrium and gone off in the wrong direction."

"Damn it!" Buck gritted his teeth. "This is a hell of a situation!"

The two of them were silent, lost in their own thoughts.

Cathy slapped the water with her feet. She looked down in the water for a moment, then faced him with an anxious look. "You don't think Mike would have deliberately let go of my wrist, do you, Buck?" she asked quietly.

"Why the hell would he do that?"

Cathy stared at him. She looked scared. "Mike and I haven't been getting along all that well. We've had a lot of arguments."

"Well, all couples have a few spats. So what?"

"It's more serious than a few spats. Mike's business hasn't been doing too well. In fact, it's been losing money for years, and well, several days ago, I told him I wanted a separation."

"Ohhhh..." Buck said slowly.

Cathy looked worried. "You know, Buck, if Mike and I divorce, he gets nothing."

Threatened, Buck raised his voice. "I know what you're thinking and just stop it, Cathy. Mike would never do anything to hurt you. Your hand probably just hit a piece of rock and Mike lost his grip on you."

Cathy sniffed softly. "I guess so."

"Look, this cave is enough to make anybody morbid.

But Lynn is still up there. She'll radio the Coast Guard. They'll send out someone to rescue us."

"She said she doesn't know how to use the radio."

"She's got a cell phone. She'll call for help. Let's just stop letting our thoughts run away from us, agreed?"

She paused. "Agreed."

"Look, I'm going to turn off the flashlight again, okay? I don't want to use any more light than we need."

"Okay."

He switched off the light again.

All in all, he felt pretty miserable. Right now, if things had worked out according to schedule, they'd be having a lobster lunch with Mike and Lynn. Instead, they were in this nasty-smelling hole. He was hungry and thirsty and he could hardly breathe.

He was trying to look at the bright side, but there was a real possibility he could die in this cave.

If he died, he wondered how Lynn would manage. He had a pretty good life insurance policy, but she still hadn't worked in a long time, and she might not be able to find decent employment. God, it would be hard on Lynn, having to take care of Scott and Kevin alone. He wondered if she'd have enough money for the kids' education. He didn't want them working at McDonald's for the rest of their lives.

Scotty was a straight-A student, a really bright kid. He could be a doctor or a scientist if he put his mind to it. And Kevin was such an outgoing, sociable little guy. He felt a pang of emptiness. He wouldn't be around to see his kids play football, or graduate from high school or go to college.

He analyzed their situation. If Mike hadn't called Search and Rescue, he and Cathy were doomed. Even then, there was the possibility the team wouldn't find them in time.

As for Lynn, she didn't know the first thing about VHF radios. She'd never had the interest to learn about diving or boats. He'd tried to teach her CPR once, but she just wouldn't do it.

Death. He was too young to die. He was only forty-five. He was just getting started in life, building his business and his place in the community. This wasn't the way it was supposed to end, suffocating in some godforsaken cave on an underwater dive expedition.

"Buck, do you believe in God?" Cathy asked.

Buck kicked the water nervously with his toes. "Look, I majored in biology, you know that, Cathy. I'm a scientist."

"Yeah, well, I just wondered what you thought about a hereafter."

He frowned. "If you're asking me if I believe in a heaven and hell, I have my doubts."

But he had to admit, her question intrigued him. He wondered if there was a hereafter. If there was, he might not go to heaven. There would be no priest to sprinkle holy water over him or say last rites. When he died, he wouldn't even have a proper burial.

At first, when he was very young, he had believed in the hereafter. The church fathers had drummed it into him. In fact, he was a devout Catholic — an altar boy — up every day at six, dressed in white robes while he paraded to the altar with a cross. He'd been proud to do the work of God.

But at age eleven, his Irish Catholic father quit his job and decided to start a restaurant business in Spain with an associate. He separated from Buck's mother, uprooted Buck and his four siblings from New York and placed them all in a Jesuit boarding school in Spain.

Buck supposed it was then that he'd lost his faith.

"You're a big boy now," his mother said, as she kissed him good-bye. "You take care of your brothers."

Although he assured his mother that he would take care of the others, he felt frightened, abandoned and rejected.

The boarding school was strange and forbidding. He was in a foreign country and everyone spoke another language. The ways of the black-robed priests, chanting hymns and performing rituals, seemed strange and anti-quated and he distrusted them.

But he was a big boy. He wasn't supposed to cry. He fought back his emotions until one day he burst into tears in the church. An old priest, Father Salinio, took his hand and led him to one of the wooden benches. "Is there anything I can help you with, my son?"

He shook his head and stared at the floor.

"Do you miss your family?" he asked.

Buck nodded. "My father promised he would come back and get me, but he hasn't."

"Your father has assured me your visit here is a short one," said the priest in a kindly voice. "Just have a little faith, my son."

But Buck didn't see any evidence of an end. Each day stretched into weeks and the weeks into months and the months into years. "He'll never take us out of here."

"That is what faith is about, my son. It is the gift of the human spirit. Let us pray to God that one day your family will be reunited."

In disbelief, Buck looked at the priest. How could you have faith when all the evidence was against you? He bowed his head, paying lip service to the priest's advice, but never really believing it.

It wasn't until he was sixteen that his parents finally

reunited and Buck and his siblings moved back to the States where his father took a job in the insurance industry.

He supposed he had been born a scientist. As a young boy, he had caught field mice and dissected them, trying to discover what made them move. He felt that all he needed to understand life was to understand the inner workings of living things. He did not need the hocus-pocus, mumbo jumbo of the priests.

Later, he decided to study biology in college. He had turned to science for answers — not God.

Yet, here in this cave with only the darkness and the water around him, he questioned his beliefs. He wondered if there was a hereafter.

Overall, he hadn't led a bad life. Sure, he'd done a few bad things — streaked across a football field in high school, smoked a little dope in college and once cheated on his taxes. But, all in all, he hadn't really hurt anybody. If there was a heaven, maybe he still had a shot at it. He sure didn't feel he deserved to go to hell.

Buck felt his mind drifting back to his youth, floating in a boat. Where was he?

When he graduated from college, he'd taken a trip to the Greek Islands with some friends. They'd gone exploring and come upon a cave. They'd all decided to search the cave and were surprised to discover people worshipping inside.

One of the local villagers, an old man in his sixties, approached them and explained they were in a church. There were windows along the sides of the cave, just holes made of stained glass, and when they went further down, they discovered icons — crucifixes and figures of Christ.

Buck hadn't realized until then that the first churches

in the world had been built in caves. It struck him as particularly odd that people would worship in such places. This only reinforced his idea that the Christian religion was filled with barbarisms and strange practices. After his visit to the cave, he internally renounced any formal type of Christianity.

Yet, here in this cave, he felt strangely uneasy, as if he was in some odd type of cathedral that led to forgotten rooms and passageways with no beginning and no end. The whole cave was an aquatic architecture of trapdoors that led nowhere.

His scientific tools, his compass and his navigation instruments were of no help to him. His logic had proved to be faulty. Even his senses were useless. He could not see. There was no sound. He couldn't even smell; his sinuses were all stopped up. He had nothing to rely on here.

Suddenly, he felt someone shaking him and he heard Cathy's voice. "Buck, Buck, wake up!"

His eyes opened into infinite blackness. The carbon dioxide buildup must have made him drift off to sleep. He knew what happened when the lungs filled with toxic CO_2 gas. Your breathing increased, sometimes you hallucinated, you lost consciousness and finally, you died. It was going to be what happened to both of them if they didn't get out of this cave.

"Buck, you were snoring," Cathy said.

"Really?" He was surprised. "Lynn tells me I don't snore." He felt his nose. The nasal passages were swollen. "My sinuses are killing me. I wonder how much time has gone by."

"I don't know," Cathy groaned. "It feels like forever. I wish someone would come and get us out of here."

"We're got to get out of here ourselves. We need to

come up with a plan." The possibility of rescue was becoming slimmer with each passing minute. Buck didn't have a watch, but several hours must have transpired since they'd first found this air pocket. He turned on his flashlight.

"What are we going to do?"

"I don't know," he said despondently. "We don't know where we are. Our navigation instruments are no good. We have nothing to rely on."

Cathy wrinkled her brow. "We have ourselves, Buck. Maybe that's enough."

"Well, do you have any ideas?"

She shook her head. "How about you?"

"I'm thinking, let me think." He pondered. Neither one of them had enough air to get out of that cave. But a diver with two tanks, that was a different story...

He looked at his console. "Cathy, how much air have you got in your tank?"

She glanced at her console. "About 700 pounds."

"I've got 600. If one of us takes both tanks, and if the vis has improved, we might be able to find our way out. It's a long shot, but it might work. What do you say?"

She hesitated. "I don't know."

"Look, Cathy, it's the only chance we've got," he argued. "We can't just sit here like a ship that's dead in the water."

She gritted her teeth. "All right, I guess you're right. But, I can't do it. My legs are still cramping up."

He paused. "Well...then I guess it's up to me to give it a shot." He hesitated. "I don't know whether I'm gonna make it."

"You've got to have faith in yourself." She smiled bravely.

He nodded. Cathy always put up a good front, even

when she was scared.

She pursed her lips. "Go for it, Buck."

"Look. I'm going to drop my lobster bag down here." He pointed straight down. "This will be the landmark in case I'm running out of air and I'm trying to find my way back." He dropped his orange Gulper game bag squeaking with lobsters. He had a sickening feeling. He might never get it back.

He glanced at Cathy. "You use your flashlight, count out about fifteen minutes and then start flashing your light in case I'm trying to find my way back. I'm only good for twenty minutes, so I'm either out by then or I'm dead."

She winced.

"After that, you'll need to flash that light five or six times every thirty seconds to let someone know you're here."

She gave him a thumbs-up. "Got it."

He released the tank from her floating vest and tucked it under his arm. "Give me your gloves. I'm going to use them to mark a path so I can find my way back."

"All right, Hansel. Wish we'd brought bread crumbs."

"Not to worry, I've got other trail markers."

She leaned over and gave him a hug. "Be careful. I'll pray for you, Buck."

"Okay, Cathy. I'm gonna need all the help I can get."

Buck took one long last look at Cathy, then silently slipped into the vast blackness of the water. It was to be either the beginning of the end for him, or a new beginning.

CHAPTER

10

EVEN WITH THE TWO tanks, Buck's life support system was limited. He had approximately twenty-five minutes at the most to find the entrance of the cave, and if he didn't, he was history.

He turned on his flashlight. The cave itself was an amorphous mass of rock with gaping holes, ravines, gouges, slithering slits and craggy openings. His compass was useless — none of these tunnels were a straight shot out. They curved and bent, went up and down, veined and fissured like capillaries branching off an artery.

He monitored his pressure gauge. His tank was already at 550. This whole escapade was going to be a shot in the dark and he had no time to pussyfoot around.

He started out quickly, making his way to an open crevice on his far left. He shone his flashlight down the recess. That one was out. He could already see the cave ending at a cul-de-sac at no more than eight feet.

Shit, this was confusing. All these crevices and cracks looked the same. He felt a little dizzy, but continued swimming until he came to another gaping hole and inspected it.

As he examined the tunnel, his perception of it seemed to change before his eyes. How odd! It looked like a giant root canal. He had the strange feeling he was in his office, starting an operation on a patient, only this time he didn't have his pathfinder, the scientific instrument he used when he was plotting out the course for a root canal. He felt lost without it. He blinked.

Was he hallucinating? There must be less air in that pocket than he'd originally surmised. He figured he was having aftereffects from the CO_2 buildup. He took a deep breath of air and let it out slowly. Afterwards, he felt better.

Which tunnel to take? He didn't know how he knew, but somehow, he felt certain this was the right tunnel. Buck had never put his trust in feelings before — he'd always gone by scientific evidence. But his feelings seemed too strong, almost overwhelming.

He shone his flashlight into the tunnel several feet, but darkness swallowed the probing beam. The tunnel was silty, indicating there had been some activity — maybe by him and Cathy.

He dropped one of Cathy's gloves at the entranceway, and swam quickly down the tunnel, staying high enough above the bottom to minimize disturbing the silt. He went another fifteen or twenty feet. The tunnel suddenly branched off in two directions. He decided to take the one to the right. He went a couple of feet, but the ceiling began to lower.

Suddenly, he scraped to a halt. He tried to wriggle forward, but he couldn't move.

He realized his tank had gotten wedged in the ceiling rock. The tunnel had narrowed and he was caught, closed in by the cave's walls. His ribs and shoulders squeezed tight against the rock.

He wriggled again, but still couldn't budge. He brought his wrist up, focusing his eyes and attention on the instruments and gauges. He was down another fifty pounds.

His heart was racing; his hands were twitching. He was breathing rapidly, bubbles roaring past his head. The air bubbles skipped along the top of the walls like some sort of strange sea creatures trying to escape.

Escape. He felt like taking the regulator out of his mouth, tearing off his tank and clawing his way to the surface. But that would be instant death. He needed his tank. Or did he?

A picture came to mind of Mike scooting up the cracks of the caves where the two had gone lobster hunting. He always left his tank at the bottom, only taking his regulator hose.

That was it! If Mike didn't need a tank, he didn't either. He could still breathe without it.

He dug down in the silt, giving himself a little more room to move. He inhaled a big breath of air, then took the regulator out of his mouth. Squirming backward as it came forward, he began pushing his tank vest up over his shoulders.

His joints felt like they were separating from their anchoring bones and his lungs felt cramped, but at last he was rewarded by a hollow thud. The tank unlocked from the ceiling with a shower of debris — bits of rock and broken shells falling over his shoulders and back.

He grabbed the hose and stuck the regulator back in his mouth, taking another gasp of air. He wriggled forward and shoved the vest, gear and both tanks ahead of him through the sticky ooze.

At his sides, jagged fossils and rocks ripped at his

suit.

He crawled along on his belly until the passageway opened up. Then he slipped his tank back on and held Cathy's cylinder under the other arm. A couple of feet more and he came back to the fork that he found earlier.

This time, he cautiously followed the other curve and directed his flashlight beam into the distance. His eyes chased the spot of light. All right! This might be it! No dead end, at least as far as he could see which was only about ten feet.

He started down the new passageway following the flashlight beam farther and farther into the tunnel, realizing that if this wasn't the right one, he was putting himself in a lot of danger. His pressure gauge had almost bottomed out.

At this point, he didn't have enough air to even get back to Cathy. All he could do was have faith that air and light lay ahead. Luckily, after approximately twenty feet, he still had a clear pathway.

Suddenly, he noticed some resistance in the regulator.

Uh, oh! His tank was about empty. The pressure gauge was on zero. He sucked in one last long breath from the regulator and jettisoned the tank.

Now painfully aware of what it felt like to run out of air, he put Cathy's regulator in his mouth. If he ran out a second time, there would be no third tank to save him. He would be dead in minutes — his own body a marker of his efforts to find his way out.

He came to another branch in the tunnel. Which way to go? He peered down the slithery crevice. One gap seemed brighter than the other. It might be an optical illusion, but he didn't have time to ponder the issue.

He glanced at his console. He had only about 350 pounds of air left, less than ten minutes.

He made for the brighter tunnel. He dropped another of Cathy's gloves. As he proceeded down the passageway, it seemed to get lighter.

Twenty feet down, he saw a speck of expanding light in the distance. He clenched his fist and tucked his elbow in silent triumph. Yes. Right on! He'd made it! He was so excited he actually peed in his suit. He was at the entranceway to the tunnel! He allowed himself one deep long glorious breath of air.

He leapt for the tunnel entrance, making for the crack of blue as if ascending to heaven from a stint in hell. He swam out of the tunnel entrance into the main chamber of the cave and into the ambient light. God, it was good to get out of the darkness. Liquid blue light rippled over his body. He sucked air in relief.

He started to slowly ascend to the surface, resisting the urge to go faster than his air bubbles. The fatal mistake of novice divers was to panic, ascending too fast, and as the air expanded in their lungs, it burst them.

He had gone fifteen feet when he felt a sudden cramp in his lungs. Instantly, he knew what was happening. Damn! He was out of the cave and more than halfway up, but he'd overestimated the air in his tank.

He looked at the console. It was almost on zero. He decided to take one large breath and go straight up, rather than trying to make his way underwater to the boat. He took his breath, watched the pressure gauge bottom out, and resisted the urge to kick frantically to the surface.

But before he reached the surface, he exhaled his last bubble of air. His lungs were on fire. Already his peripheral vision was starting to fade. Was he losing consciousness? Would he die before reaching the surface?

He gagged, breathing in seawater. He resisted the

urge to propel himself upward like a missile. Slowly, me-
thodically, he moved up, up, up from this watery grave
until suddenly, just when he felt like all was lost, he broke
the surface.

Air! He spat out Cathy's regulator and took a huge
gasp of glorious air! Air! He took in large gulps, sucking
in what his body craved. He saw blue skies and clouds
overhead and sea gulls flying. He heard the barks of
seals. He smelled sea spray and felt wind hitting his face.

Hallelujah! Praise be! He was born again!

He looked around and saw the boat's fiberglass hull,
no more than fifty feet away, gently rising and dipping in
the afternoon waves.

"Lynn!" he shouted, waving frantically. "Lynn!"

He waved and shouted again and again. He saw
Lynn and Mike on the flybridge of the boat. Thank God!
Mike was alive! Mike and Lynn were alive. He was alive!
He laughed out loud. God, it felt good to be alive!

Mike and Lynn waved.

"Hey, over here!" Buck yelled. He inflated his BC with
his mouth, then put his snorkel between his lips and swam
to the boat.

Mike hurried down the ladder to the cockpit of the
boat, followed by Lynn.

Buck grasped the dive ladder with one hand and
Mike's hand with the other.

"Goddamn, Buck!" Mike shouted. "Jesus, am I glad
to see you! I've been down in that cave looking for you
and Cathy for over an hour. Where's Cathy?"

Buck put one foot on the dive ladder. "She's still in the
cave," he panted, as he climbed up. "We've gotta get
her out!"

Lynn dashed up to him, threw her arms around his
neck and hugged him. "I was so worried, Buck. We

thought you were dead."

Ecstatic, Buck hugged her back.

He dropped his weight belt as Mike helped him with his tank. He managed to pull off his fins and stagger across the deck.

Suddenly, the two figures dizzily whirled around him in a frenzied dance. He blinked. Afraid he would lose consciousness, he leaned against the salon door.

Mike grasped him by the shoulders. "What do you mean Cathy's still down there. Where's my wife?"

"Now calm down, buddy," Buck said, coughing and hacking as he tried to get his breath.

"Did you leave her down there by herself?"

"Just hold on, Mike."

"I don't understand. What's going on? Where is she? She's not dead, is she?"

"She's okay." Buck pulled away. "Cathy's okay."

His head felt like it had been hammered against a brick wall. "Let me get my breath, will you?" Buck said. "Jesus Christ!" He paused and filled his lungs with air. "We found some sort of gigantic air pocket. Like the one in the back of the chamber, only larger." He coughed and heaved. "She's got enough air, at least for the moment."

"We've gotta get her out, Doc," Mike said. "Give me the details. How much air do you think Cathy's got?"

Buck unzipped his wet suit. He flopped down on a chair in his swim trunks, grabbed a towel and buried his head in it. "Hard to tell. Maybe an hour or two."

"She still got her tank?"

Buck shook his head. "I had to use both tanks to get out. I told her I'd get help, get her out." He was still gasping for air. He bristled. "What the fuck happened, Mike? Where the hell were you?"

"Me? I've been looking for you guys for over an hour in that cave! I ran a line down and took extra tanks, but I had no luck. Jesus Christ, you guys scared the shit out of me. I thought you were dead!"

Buck shook his head. "Cathy said you let go of her hand!"

Mike exploded. "I didn't let go of her hand! Hell, she let go of me. I felt my hand hit a rock, and then she let go, and before I knew it, I'd lost her! You two scared the hell out of me, man!"

Buck sighed in relief. He'd been right about his buddy all along. It was only logical. Cathy's hand had hit a rock.

Mike sat down next to him and put his head in his hand. "I tried to find you, but I started bumping into rocks, going in different directions. I finally found my way out of the cave. I came back, got a couple of extra tanks and ran a line down. That's when I discovered that tunnel branching off the main chamber. I tried to find you, but...I had no luck. I ran out of air myself. Shit, that cave is a death trap." He gazed at Buck.

Buck nodded. "We've got to go back down and get her out."

"Man, what do you think I've been doing all this time? But I ran out of tanks. I had to surface."

Buck felt his heart skip a beat. "You ran out of tanks?" he repeated in shock.

"Yeah. I used up a couple trying to find you. I ran one spare one down there, but we haven't got any extra tanks on board."

Buck grimaced. "Oh, shit!" They'd never get Cathy out of the cave if they didn't have enough tanks. "We've got to do something, buddy. She'll die down there. We've got to radio the Coast Guard."

"I already did," Mike shouted. He shook his head. "But, they'll never get here in time. They're way back in Oxnard. We need help NOW!"

Buck threw his towel down on the chair in frustration. He put his head in his hands. "Goddamn!" he said. Mike was probably right.

Suddenly, he remembered Pete Kendall. "Hey, Pete's got tanks. He's at Chinese Beach and he knows this cave. Why don't we radio him? He'll help out...that is, if he's not plastered."

Mike nodded. "Let's give Pete a shot, Doc. He's all we've got right now."

Mike led the way to the lower helm station, followed by Lynn.

"How long do you think it will take Pete to get here?" Lynn asked.

"About forty-five minutes," Mike answered.

Lynn wrinkled her forehead. "Do you think forty-five minutes is too long? How long can she last, Buck?"

Buck shook his head. "I don't know, honey."

Leaning against Lynn as she tried to steady his walk, Buck stumbled after Mike. He fell into a chair as soon as they were inside.

Mike sat down in front of the VHF radio, punched up channel 68 and keyed the mike.

"*Paramour, Paramour,* this is *Trident.* Do you read me?"

There was a crackle and then a voice came over the radio. It sounded tinny. "This is *Paramour,* Mike. What's up?"

Mike leaned forward. "We need your ass over here, pronto."

"Ah, my ass is occupied."

"Hey, buddy, this is no time to joke," Mike argued. "We need your help."

"What's up?" Pete asked.

"We've got an emergency, Pete. Cathy's trapped in an underwater cave. We need extra tanks. There's a limited supply of air. She could die."

"Jesus! Why didn't you say so, buddy? Okay, I'll be there ASAP. Where are you located?"

"We're off the front side of the island, in the first cove west of Painted Cave. Get your ass over here quick."

"I'm on my way. Out."

Mike released the button. "We got him." He leaned back in his chair.

Buck wiped his hand across his brow in relief.

Lynn put her hand on Buck's shoulder. "You think you can find her again, honey?"

Buck squeezed her hand. "Maybe. I left a trail. A bug bag, a couple of tanks, a glove. I might be able to locate her if the silt has cleared up."

"What are the chances of that?"

Buck wrinkled his brow. "It's hard to tell. The silt takes a long time to settle. A couple of hours, at least. Let's just hope it doesn't cover up the trail."

"Yeah," Mike agreed. "What do you say we get our gear together?"

They hurried outside to the cockpit. In the distance, the mountainous cliffs of Santa Cruz Island rose green and brown into the sky. Up above, sea gulls circled. The water lapped gently against the hull as the boat strained on the anchor.

Buck's eyes swept the water. Oh hell, the surge was picking up.

Down below, Cathy was waiting.

"I hope we get there in time!" Buck exclaimed.

Mike thumped him on the shoulder. "We'll do it, Doc. We'll get her out. Right now, all we can do is wait for

Pete."

    As he quickly grabbed his gear, Buck gritted his teeth. "Yeah, I guess that's all we can do — hurry up and wait."

CHAPTER

11

THE COAST GUARD CUTTER *Halibut*, out of Marina del
Rey, was proceeding southeast at approximately thirteen
knots. The *Halibut* had just come off rescuing a forty-foot
Tolleycraft that had struck a buoy. The crew had been out
twelve hours and they were tired. They were headed back
to the marina.

At the helm, Petty Officer First Class William Andrews
switched his VHF radio from the distress channel 16 to a
scan mode. His radio had a high-gain antenna that allowed it to pick up conversations between boaters from
as far away as thirty miles.

Suddenly, the scan stopped on channel 68. Between
bursts of squelch noise, fragments of voices broke through.

"...we've got an emergency, Pete. Cathy's trapped in
an underwater cave. We need extra tanks. There's a limited supply of air. She could die."

Another weak signal carried bits of a second voice
through the air. "Jesus! Why didn't you say so, buddy?
Okay, I'll be there ASAP."

Andrews felt the hair on his neck stand on end. "Uh, oh," he said. "Looks like a dive incident in the making."

"We'd better get a bearing," answered John Hawkins, standing beside him at the wheel.

Andrews nodded, instantly flipping a switch to put the radio receiver in direction-finder mode, which allowed him to determine the straight-line bearing of the boater's radio signal. The bearing was 280° true from the *Halibut's* position. He quickly switched back to a communication mode.

Voices broke in over the radio. "Bring extra line."

"Will do. Where are you located?"

"We're off the front side of the island, one cove west of Painted Cave. Get your ass over here quick."

Andrews keyed the mike. "Break, break. Divers in distress, this is the United States Coast Guard cutter *Halibut* on channel 68. Do you need assistance? Over."

There was just more static on the frequency. Probably, the antennas on the dive boat weren't strong enough to pick up the Coast Guard signals from as far away as Marina del Rey.

"Try it again," Hawkins said, leaning over anxiously.

Andrews repeated his message. "Break, break. Vessels conversing at Painted Cave, Santa Cruz Island. This is the United States Coast Guard cutter *Halibut* at Marina del Rey. Give your position and the number of persons in distress. Over."

There was no answer.

"Damn!" Andrews rapped his fist on his knee. He screwed up his face and pondered the situation. He was out of luck in notifying the divers. But it was the Coast Guard's duty to send out a search and rescue team when there was a vessel in distress.

Andrews put down the mike. "Take the wheel, will

you, Hawkins? I'm going to notify the lieutenant."

Hawkins switched places with Andrews.

Andrews opened the door to the deck and walked down the steps.

Lieutenant Roger Bainbridge, a tall man with tanned weatherworn skin and deep blue eyes, was standing at the rail of the *Halibut* and gazing out to sea. He had a styrofoam cup of coffee in his hand.

"Lieutenant," Andrews shouted, approaching Bainbridge.

Lieutenant Bainbridge squinted as he turned to face him. He had small crow's feet around his eyes and his eyelids sagged. "What is it?" he asked, wearily.

"We've got an emergency — a group of divers in distress."

The lieutenant ran his hand through his greying hair. "Did they give you their location?"

"No, sir. I was monitoring channel 68 when I heard part of their distress call. They were radioing a friend. I called them, but they must be too far away to hear us."

"Did you get a bearing?"

"They're at 280° true from our position. They said one diver was trapped in a cave in the first cove west of Painted Cave."

"They're off Santa Cruz Island. We're too far to get to them. You'd better radio Channel Islands. See if another cutter is somewhere in the vicinity."

Andrews nodded, then rushed back to the pilot house. He crossed to the control panel, switched the frequency for the Coast Guard station at Channel Islands Harbor and spoke into the mike. "This is the U.S. Coast Guard cutter *Halibut*. Over."

There was the sound of static and then a voice responded. "*Halibut*, this is the Coast Guard station, Channel Islands. Go ahead. Over."

"We have a group of cave divers in distress. At least one, possibly more divers trapped in a cave the first cove west of Painted Cave. Is another cutter in the vicinity?"

"Affirmative, *Halibut.* We've got the *Blackfin* in open water. We can radio her to change course."

"Can you get a search and rescue team out here? Over."

"Will do, *Halibut.* Can you give a description of the vessels?"

"Negative. We weren't able to contact the vessel. Over."

"They weren't on the distress channel?"

"Negative. We picked them up on channel 68. They were radioing a friend for help."

"All right, *Halibut.* We'll get on it."

"Thanks, Station. Out."

The Channel Islands Harbor Coast Guard station at Oxnard occupied a small two-story brick building, a spit away from the water. Petty Officer Dave Fawcett had a window view of the water and the fishing boats tied at the slips. He also had a good view of Oxnard Harbor's breakwater and jetties. Across from the station were condominiums — some, stucco with terra-cotta roofs; others with rustic fronts.

Fawcett turned away from the window to face Petty Officer Ron Jones seated at the desk next to him.

Jones swiveled around in his chair. "Another dive incident in those caves off Santa Cruz Island?"

"Yeah," Fawcett said.

"Oh, shit!" Jones muttered, under his breath. "We just pulled two out a month ago. Been dead at least two weeks. Dive crews get the heebie-jeebies in those caves."

"Yeah, tell me about it," Fawcett nodded. He picked up the phone beside him and dialed the direct number of the Central Receiving Commander at the Ventura County Sheriff's Department.

A male voice came on the line. "Captain John Gilbert, here."

"Hey, John, it's Dave."

"Yeah, Dave, what's up?"

Fawcett shoved the phone under his neck. "We've got a dive incident off Santa Cruz Island. Divers trapped in a cave one cove west of Painted Cave. We need a rescue team to transport to the island."

There was a pause. "Okay, I'll call Search and Rescue. Do you have a boat?"

"We can have the Blackfin at the Santa Barbara Marina in an hour," Fawcett said. Fawcett glanced at his watch. "How much time will it take to get a team in the water?"

"I'll get back with you on that."

Fawcett put down the phone. Then, he radioed the Blackfin and ordered her to proceed to the Santa Barbara Harbor. When he was finished, he got up and grabbed his binoculars. He went to the window.

Off in the distance, Fawcett could see the jutting, rugged cliffs of Santa Cruz Island. He turned around to Jones. "You know, I can't even remember the last time we pulled a live one out of those caves."

Jones took a sip of his coffee, then tossed the cup in the trash can. "I do. We've never pulled out a live one."

Captain Gilbert, the watch commander on duty, acted as the central receiver for the entire police force by rerouting calls to the proper sections of the sheriff's department. He was enclosed in an office on the basement floor of the four-story building occupied by the Ventura County Sheriff's Department. No one but him was aware of the emergency.

He immediately reached across his desk cluttered with piles of papers and several styrofoam coffee cups, and picked up the phone to dial Sergeant Rick Humphries who was in charge of all operations for Search and Rescue.

Search and Rescue consisted of sea, air and land operations. Although the rest of the unit referred to themselves as Search and Rescue, the dive unit had named themselves Search and Recovery, because they'd never pulled a live body out of the caves on the Channel Islands.

Captain Gilbert waited for a moment until Humphries picked up the phone. "Sergeant Humphries."

"Captain Gilbert, here."

"What's up?"

"There's a dive incident in progress off Santa Cruz Island. Divers trapped in a cave one cove west of Painted Cave. Can you ready up a team?"

"Can do. You got a cutter?"

"The *Blackfin*. She'll pick up your crew and transport them to the island. She's due in at the Santa Barbara Harbor at 1500."

"We'll be there," Humphries said.

"What are we looking at as far as time?" asked Gilbert.

"Probably three hours to get a team in the water."

"That may be too late."

"It's the best we can do," huffed Humphries, hanging up the phone.

Sergeant Rick Humphries, a middle-aged man who had seen more than his share of dive accidents, swept his hand through his thick brown hair. He rarely had emergencies, but when he did, he had to act quickly.

Humphries usually used a paging system to call the volunteers, but this type of rescue would be difficult. He needed specialized equipment and a team, all too heavy to transport via helicopter. He also needed experienced volunteers who knew those caves and the conditions on the islands. He had four volunteers with those qualifications on call today, ready to act at a moment's notice.

Humphries immediately got on the phone. His lead team member was Johnny Bailey, who owned The Dive Shop in Camarillo. He phoned the shop, waiting while it rang several times.

"The Dive Shop." He recognized the voice. It was Gertrude Tilman, Johnny's office manager.

"Gertrude, Sergeant Humphries here," he said. "Is Johnny around?"

"Sure. He's with a customer, just a minute." She paused. "Hey, Johnny!" she shouted. "Pick up the outside line. It's Sergeant Humphries."

He heard the click of another phone being picked up and then Johnny's voice. "You'll like that mask," Johnny yelled. "It's a Scubapro. One of the best on the market. But don't take my word for it. Try it on." He paused. "Yeah, Rick, what's up?"

"We've got a dive incident."

"Uh, oh," Johnny said. "Where are we headed?"

"Santa Cruz Island."

"You got a cutter?"

"Yeah, the *Blackfin* is due in at 1500. We'll have a patrol car run you out to the Santa Barbara Marina. Be down at the station ASAP."

"Okay, Sergeant," Johnny said. "I'm on my way."

Sergeant Humphries hung up the phone. He proceeded

to put in calls to the next three team members. But while he was doing so, his mind jumped ahead.

He analyzed the situation. Recently, two novice divers had been killed off Santa Cruz Island. Search and Rescue hadn't been able to save them in time and he'd gotten a lot of bad press over the incident. He couldn't afford another failed rescue mission in less than a month. The reputation of his team would be riding on this operation.

What the press didn't realize was that the caves at Santa Cruz weren't a standard rescue operation. The people they were trying to rescue could already be dead by the time they reached the island.

Then, once the rescue team was in the water, they had to contend with the surge — a powerful long-acting wave of water running below the surface that could thrust a body around like a Ping-Pong ball. With just a weak surge of two knots a top-notch swimmer would get pushed backwards. But a strong surge could slam a body into rock walls, and the surge at the Channel Islands could get tremendous in the afternoon. Divers could be killed.

By the time his team got to Santa Cruz, it would be nightfall. Night diving was especially tough. There was the problem of visibility. Then there were the sharks that fed on the baby seals. Although sharks didn't usually attack humans, they failed to differentiate between a human limb and a baby seal. One day he'd been spear fishing with a friend off the islands when a mako had attacked them. He'd escaped, but his friend had lost a leg.

All in all, he'd have to prepare his rescue team for the worst.

CHAPTER

12

"HAND ME THAT SCREWDRIVER, will you Jeff?" Pete pushed back a rivulet of sweat from his brow. He retrieved a white terry cloth towel from a storage cabinet and wiped his face.

Jeff Wagner reached in the tool box next to him and grabbed a screwdriver, handing it to Pete.

"There, that ought to do it." Pete tightened the last screw, stood up and pushed the ignition switch. Nothing happened.

"I don't believe this!" Pete said. He'd just bought the *Paramour* three months ago. It was one of the best production sports fishing boats in its class. He looked around its modern profile with its enclosed bridge, four staterooms with full heads, a spacious salon/galley arrangement and huge tournament-style cockpit, and wondered why the hell his new two-million dollar boat wouldn't start.

"Looks like both motors are dead," Jeff said. "It's got to be an electrical problem."

"Shit!" Pete threw his towel on the deck in frustration.

"Now what the hell am I gonna do? Cathy's trapped in a cave and this damned boat won't start."

"Hey, calm down, buddy. Don't sweat it. Take the *Vagabond*."

Pete glanced at Jeff's boat. The *Vagabond* was an Ocean 53 Motor Yacht. She wasn't a dive boat. She had a huge fully extended main salon running all the way to the transom. She didn't have a swim ladder or platform, but rather a removable boarding ladder that attached to the side rail. Without the ladder in place, it was impossible to board her from the water. She had to be boarded by a sort of gang plank on land or be lashed to another boat in open water. He supposed since they'd be diving off Mike's boat, it didn't really matter.

Pete glanced at his buddy. "Thanks, Jeff."

"No problem. I'll give you a hand with the gear."

The two transferred tanks, rope and diving gear from the *Paramour* to the foredeck of Jeff's motor yacht. Once all the equipment had been assembled on the *Vagabond*, Jeff launched the Zodiac, a small inflatable rubber boat.

"You sure you don't need an extra hand?" Jeff asked, preparing to board the Zodiac. "I'll be glad to help out, buddy." He grabbed the picnic lunch Judy had prepared for the group — avocados, cold cuts, the works.

"Naw," Pete said, a little despondent. He'd been looking forward to that lunch. "I'll be fine." Jeff and Judy weren't divers, so Jeff wouldn't be much use to him on this rescue mission. "Anyway, somebody needs to stay here. You think you can keep an eye on the babes while I'm gone?"

"Oh, don't worry about that, buddy." Jeff winked with some amusement. "I haven't taken my eyes off them all day."

"Yeah, I noticed," Pete said sarcastically.

Wistfully, Pete stood at the rail and stared at the three gorgeous beauties lying on a small strip of sandy beach, only fifty yards from his boat. They were oiling their half-clad topless bodies.

Jeff had already taken care of the girls — mainly by supplying them with the drinks he carried in his cooler. Damn, Pete thought. He hadn't come closer to heaven than this in a long time. If they kept drinking, they'd probably be completely unclad.

Next to the babes was Judy. A leftover hippie from the sixties, Judy had once joined a nudist colony in addition to her other activities which consisted mainly of studying yoga and astrology. He supposed that's why she preferred the more deserted beaches like this one to Arroyo Burro, Henry's or Goleta, the standard hangouts of most Santa Barbarans.

Pete oogled the babes — Delores, the brunette; Diane, the redhead; and Candie, the blonde, or was it Mandie? Well, what was a name anyway when she had boobs like those?

Pete watched Jeff start the motor of the Zodiac. Damn, Cathy had picked a hell of a time to get trapped in a cave. Yet, he figured he'd have enough time when he got back to do some serious lovemaking if the girls stayed happy and well-plied with Jeff's booze.

Regretfully, he turned away from the scene and started the engine. He untied the two boats, activated the windlass and weighed anchor. Then he pulled back on the throttle and maneuvered the Vagabond out of the cove.

Once he was in open water, Pete brought the Vagabond up to full cruising speed — about twenty-three knots. He glanced at his watch. With luck, he could probably make it back to the beach in three or four hours.

As the Vagabond made her way out of Chinese Harbor, Pete pondered his situation. He'd told Mike and Buck he had explored that cave. But, the truth was he knew nothing about it. He'd said he dived it because he didn't want to appear second-rate in front of a hotshot diver like Mike Gallagher.

The fact was, Pete didn't even know there was another cave next to Painted Cave. He'd explored a few caves on the south side of the island, but none on the north. Shit! He supposed he would have to own up in front of Mike and Buck.

He frowned as he contemplated the situation. It was easy to get lost in those caves. They formed an elaborate, sometimes interconnecting labyrinth underneath the island. Their tunnels could go deep into subterranean depths, plunging a diver without a light into Stygian darkness. If a dive line was broken or cut, the diver would be lost forever.

Once, Pete had been exploring a cave for mapping purposes. They'd run 400 feet of dive line back without ever reaching the end. Cathy could be anywhere in that cave and it wouldn't be easy locating her.

The caves on the northwest side of the island, where Mike and Buck were located, were exposed to extraordinary hydraulic stresses. From October to June, they were okay during the morning, but after that, the caves were risky to enter. Swells running from the northwest could crash into a diver with tremendous force, smacking him into the walls at such an incredible speed that if he came out alive, he looked like he'd been in an automobile wreck.

Most of the caves had an amplifying effect on prevailing swell levels, since the passages tended to go from wide to narrow. They could suck a diver right inside and trap him forever.

He and some friends had once been placed in a life and death struggle to escape from a cave on the west end during a two-foot swell. His two friends had entered a cave during a lull period. He swam inside to join them, and was climbing up on a wide shelf near the rear of the cave when a huge swell came bouncing off the walls and ceiling, knocking them around like bowling pins.

The conditions of the caves were so violent that few species of animals could live in them. A few seals or seabirds could be found in the aboveground caves, but those below the water were inhabited by animals that could permanently attach themselves to the walls like barnacles, rock mussels, sea stars, urchins and the lobsters who held onto the rock with their claws.

Not long ago, he'd read in the *News-Press* about some bodies the Coast Guard had pulled up from Santa Cruz Island. He wasn't surprised that an experienced diver like Mike Gallagher had run into some trouble in these caves. He'd known other experienced divers who had actually ended up corpses. Anyway, Mike was known among his dive buddies for being somewhat of a daredevil. Mike was not the kind to let a cave scare him off, especially if he was hunting bugs.

Pete was feeling a little apprehensive about the rescue, although he'd never admit it to Buck or Mike. It was already one o'clock. The sharks would be on the prowl about five o'clock. Their feeding time started at dark, and by twilight, the water would be frequented by foraging makos, blues and sometimes a great white.

The whole escapade gave Pete a queasy feeling. This was really a job for the Coast Guard. Mike should have notified them. They could get a team of professional divers, even if they would arrive a little late. Pete didn't mind helping out, but he wasn't equipped with communications backups, linesmen, a whole crew and medics.

Pete suspected he knew why Mike wouldn't want to notify the Coast Guard. They'd have to call Search and Rescue in Camarillo. They would send a team out and they would start asking all kinds of questions. It could sure be embarrassing for Mike to admit that the wife of a top-notch NAUI instructor had gotten lost.

If Search and Rescue came out, the newspaper and TV reporters would be hot on their tails, asking even more questions. He supposed people would be milling around the marina, just waiting for the Coast Guard cutter to dock with the survivors. They would certainly create a buzz.

The dive accident would be all over Santa Barbara by tomorrow evening. Gossip traveled fast in its small town atmosphere. Pete should know. He spread most of it around.

Pete could see the newspaper headlines now — "Dive Instructor Loses Wife In Cave." This little escapade wasn't going to help Mike's reputation. Yeah, he suspected Mike was going to have a hard time explaining this one away.

But what if Cathy died in this cave? Then Mike was going to have to deal with more than just newspaper reporters. He'd been on a number of dives with the Ventura County Sheriff's Department. They did thorough investigations of every dive accident. They'd be all over his case.

Cathy — trapped in a cave. What a fuck-up! He thought about his first wife, Sue. Like Cathy, she was also a diver. A shame he hadn't left her down in a cave. He was paying a fortune to her in child support and alimony.

Of course, he didn't want anything to happen to Cathy. She was a great gal. But if Mike Gallagher had to call in Pete to help him out of a jam, it would sure bring Mike down a notch or two, and make Pete look like something of a hero in Santa Barbara. He could really take advantage of this situation.

Pete pictured himself as the center of every newspaper reporter's attention. He imagined the television exposure. "I'm here with Pete Kendall," a gorgeous young woman would say to the audience. "Kendall, a Santa Barbara dive instructor, performed a heroic feat today as he rescued Cathy Gallagher, the wife of former top SEAL Mike Gallagher. Mr. Gallagher lost his wife in an underwater cave."

Yeah, thought Pete, wrinkling his brow. This rescue was dangerous, but what the heck? It was worth the attention he would get from the press. He smiled deviously. This was just the opportunity Pete had been waiting for — a chance to show up Mike Gallagher.

CHAPTER

13

"1, 2, 3, 4, 5..." CATHY STARTED counting the seconds again. She huddled up in the corner of the cave with her knees between her chest. "7, 8, 9, 10..."

She gave herself a punch in the ribs with her elbow. "Slow down, Cathy. You're going too fast." She was speeding up the count. Here, in this cave she had no sense of time unless she used her own mental powers. Time was nonexistent in this watery blackness. "11, 12, 13, 14..."

Yet, time was of utmost importance. Every second meant life or death. She wished she knew the time. But she hadn't worn her dive watch. She hadn't wanted to scratch the crystal on the rocks, so she'd left it on the boat.

Counting the seconds, she hoped to estimate how long Buck had been gone, and how long it would take for a rescue team.

"58, 59, 60..." Forty-five minutes had passed. Buck had either made it to the boat and was getting help, or he had run out of air and died in this twisted tunnel.

If Buck didn't make it out, she, too, would die. No one knew where she was.

She started flashing her light as a signal, in case a rescue crew was looking for her. She switched on the light and then switched it off, over and over again for ten minutes. Then she turned it off and waited for awhile. She started the process again. On and off, on and off.

Nothing happened. There was no sound. There was no light, but her flashlight. On and off, on and off. What if the batteries gave out? What then? How would anyone find her?

There was no marker except for that orange nylon bag at the bottom of the cave floor. A nylon bag with a bunch of lobster trying to get out. Trapped. She and the lobsters. Trapped.

Was Mike alive? Was he looking for her? Or had he left her here to die?

She sighed. How could two people who were so in love, drift so far apart? What had happened to them over the years?

She thought about the series of events that had torn them apart — the failed business, the affair and finally, the loss of Jonathan. But it was more than that...it went deeper. She supposed, like all couples, they had changed.

Even before she had decided to stay at home with Jonathan, she had grown tired of the trips. Another empty hotel room, another tropical island. Guests to entertain on the boat. The same old stories from Mike. The endless roll of ocean waves. The constant shrieks of sea birds overhead. The infinite call to adventure.

One night, she stood on the deck of the boat by herself and looked up at the stars, searching. She wanted something more. She realized she had changed. But Mike had never come out of the jungles of 'Nam.

She looked out to the sea and up to the stars and felt lost in the vastness of it all. She felt cut off from everything. She wanted a place in the world, a sense of community. She missed Santa Barbara and her friends. She wanted a family, children, a home. She wanted something she could call her own. She grew restless. She was drifting away from Mike.

Nine years ago, she'd bought the home in Santa Barbara for investment purposes, but she'd grown more attached to it over time. She'd spent two years decorating it.

Then she had wanted to start a family. Cathy had thought she'd never be able to have children. But, as if by a miracle, she'd gotten pregnant. She'd been ecstatic.

When Jonathan was born, he'd been the light of her life. She remembered his large blue eyes staring up at her. She felt such peace nursing him, a sense of fulfillment in her life. She listened for the sound of cooing in his crib.

Later, when he grew older, she relished his laughter throughout the house, and the patter of his tiny feet up and down the stairs. And then, one day, the house was strangely quiet. There were no more sounds of a child in the house. It seemed empty without him.

She missed him terribly. She wanted to try again to have children. But Mike hadn't been interested.

Over the years, she'd learned Mike wasn't much of a homebody. He could stick around Santa Barbara for a month or so, but he was always restless. He had to be on the go. After sitting in front of a TV for several nights, he'd get irritable, pick fights with her. Sometimes, she was almost grateful when he would finally leave for another dive trip.

She felt years ago that if the Navy had offered him a tent in some godforsaken place fighting rebel terrorists instead of a cushy job in D.C., he would have jumped at the opportunity. Instead, he'd opted out of the service, started his dive business and married her.

It had been a gradual thing, their alienation, so subtle that she hardly realized it. A series of events, of patterns — a failing business, an affair, their child dying, and then, just life itself — all these things had finally created an insurmountable gap. Before she knew it, they had drifted apart. They were uneasy in each other's presence, trying to pretend like things were right when they weren't.

One night, not long ago, she had tried to talk with him about their marriage. He'd just come back from one of his dive trips. She fixed a special dinner by candlelight. They relaxed; they made love. Afterwards, they both lay back in bed, staring at the ceiling.

She turned to face him and smiled. "That was nice."

He fingered a strand of her blonde hair and then looked away from her. She knew he was thinking of other places, other times, perhaps other women.

She frowned. "I don't know what's happened to us, Mike."

"What do you mean?"

"I don't know," she said. "I wish I knew what was on your mind. We never talk anymore."

"What do you want to talk about?"

"Us. Our feelings."

"So talk."

She wrinkled her brow. "What happened to us, Mike? We used to be so good together. Now everything is just..."

"Just what?"

"You seem so distant."

"I'm here," he protested. "I'm right here."

She shook her head. "You're not here. You might as well be on one of your trips. I feel like you've left me."

"Oh, Cathy," he said.

"I don't want to ever lose you," she said, holding him tightly.

He snuggled against her. "Why do you think you'll lose me?"

"I don't know. Hold me."

He kissed her and held her tight. She sighed in desperation. "You've fallen out of love with me."

He pulled her to him. "That's not so, Cathy. I love you, hon."

She shook her head. He always said the right things, but she felt he didn't mean them. Somewhere along the way, she'd lost Mike.

Her mind returned to the present. She bowed her head. She and Mike had been letting go for a long time. It hadn't just started in this cave. Maybe this trip was just the culmination of it all. It was the end of all the arguments, all the disappointments in their marriage. It was the end of their passion.

She remembered what her father had said — that Mike was a killer. She'd known what he'd done in Vietnam. Was killing a Vietnamese so much different from killing one's wife?

In a way, she thought it might be easier. He didn't have to pull a trigger on a gun. There would be no blood or bones. All he had to do was just let go, swim away and never look back. It was so easy, so neat, so clean.

Perhaps she was letting her imagination run away with her. Here in this cave, with only the darkness and the wet and the cold, it was easy to let one's fears get in the way of reality. It was easy to suspect the worst. Just because they had become estranged didn't make Mike a murderer.

How could you kill someone that you had been with

all those years, that shared all those memories, the same sorrows, the same pleasures? He must still have feelings for her; she still had feelings for him. Maybe he really did still love her. Why did she doubt him so much?

Maybe Mike was searching for her in these caverns, running out of air himself. Or maybe, like her, he had become trapped.

What if they dragged her out of this cave alive and Mike was dead? Then what?

Her mind was wandering, imagining too many things, conjuring up the worst. She was losing track with reality, drifting off into another world. All these thoughts of her marriage had nothing to do with getting out of this cave. She had to concentrate on the here and now, not dwell in all these memories.

Right now, more than anything, she had to concentrate on flashing this light. On and off, on and off. She flashed it for five minutes, then turned it off. She'd give it a rest for awhile. She couldn't use up the batteries. Once the batteries were dead, she would be as good as dead also.

She stretched out for a moment and let her foot slip into the water. She shivered. The water was chilly. Luckily, it was still warm from September — probably about 70 degrees. If it was any later in the year, it would be a lot colder, and she could die.

One of the dangers in staying in the water for a long period of time was hypothermia. The body core temperature could drop. People died from it. She wondered how long she could take this loneliness and darkness and cold without freaking out.

What was that? She jerked. Something had nipped at her foot. She gripped the rocks to stop herself from falling into the water.

She turned the flashlight on. Was there something alive in this cave? She peered into the water. Nothing. Not even a fish.

She shone the flashlight beam into the water again. Was something moving in the rocks? Yes! There was something down there. Was it Buck, Mike? She bent down closer, her head almost touching the water.

There it was again! Something moved! She shone the beam in the direction.

A horrible grey wrinkled mug with a sour frown poked out from the crevices below the surface. Two yellow eyes stared menacingly up at her.

Startled, she shrieked at the top of her lungs and almost dropped the flashlight into the water. She tried to get her balance to keep from falling off the ledge. Her heart thumped like crazy.

Stupid, she thought. Stop it! She was scaring herself to death. All she'd seen was a wolf eel. It was harmless — just playing hide and seek and poking its head out of the water once in awhile. Still, it was probably the ugliest thing she had ever seen. Quasimodo's cousin, for sure.

She waited until it had gone. Then she cut off the flashlight. She had to conserve the light. She sat in the darkness for a good fifteen minutes.

She yawned, stretched and almost slipped into the water. If she wanted to float in the water, she could use her BC. But there was danger in floating. With the higher levels of CO_2, she could doze off, sink into the water and drown in her sleep.

She had no idea how many minutes had passed. It could have been ten or twenty or an hour, for that matter. Why couldn't she keep counting, keep track of the time? Was her mind so foggy? The CO_2 buildup must be clouding her thinking. She couldn't concentrate on anything.

On and off, on and off. She felt so drowsy. The pace of her breathing was growing more rapid. She knew what that meant. The CO_2 was increasing. There wasn't enough oxygen for her to survive. She was going to die.

She could think of worse ways of dying. A car wreck or a gun shot. At least this would be a rather peaceful death.

She stiffened in fear. She didn't want to die in this cave alone. She wanted someone with her. Mike. Buck. Her father. Anyone, just someone to comfort her or hold her.

She rammed her back against the rock and the pain shot through her spine to her neck. She was determined not to fall asleep and die. She'd keep herself awake through pain if she had to. On and off, on and off. It was time to turn the flashlight off again.

Mike, Buck, anybody, I need you, she thought. Where the hell are you guys?

CHAPTER

14

Buck shaded his eyes with his hand. From where he stood on the bridge, he could discern the white hull of Jeff's motor yacht in open water. It cut through the choppy whitecaps and proceeded due west toward them.

"All right, Mike!" he shouted. "Pete's here."

Buck hurried down the flybridge. Lynn was standing at the stern, peering out at Pete's boat.

The sound of the motor blasted through the air, cutting out the roars of the sea lions and the shrieks of the sea gulls. The *Vagabond* eased in closer and then slowly came alongside. The roar lulled to a steady drone as Pete brought the engines to a low idle.

"Hey, Mike!" Buck thundered. "Pete's here. What the hell's keeping you? Get your ass out here!"

Mike clambered out of the galley. He approached Buck at the cockpit. "Goddamn. Wouldn't you know it? Cathy stashed the batteries to my dive light in the wrong drawer."

"Well, does it work?"

Mike flipped on the light. "It's A-OK." He flashed Buck a thumbs-up and stowed the light on his weight belt.

"Yo!" Pete shouted, waving at them. Pete cut the engines, then walked onto the deck. He anchored next to the *Trident* and tossed them a line. "Hey, you guys, get the line, will you?" yelled Pete, cupping his hand to his mouth.

Buck grabbed the line and pulled the stern of the *Vagabond* over to the *Trident's* stern.

"Damn, are we glad to see you!" Mike shouted.

Pete grinned. "Guys, I hope this is a good one. I had to ditch three hot gorgeous babes for you two ugly bubbas." He winked at Buck.

"Where's the *Paramour*?" Buck asked.

"Ah, the motors are dead," Pete said, waving his hand. Puzzled, he turned to Mike. "So buddy, what happened to Cathy? How did she get lost?"

"Vis got bad with the silt," Mike explained. "We got separated. Cathy's stuck in some sort of air pocket."

Pete raised his eyebrow. "Damn, I bet you didn't take a tether, huh?"

Mike's face flushed bright red. "We didn't think we needed one. We thought it was one big chamber."

"Boy, is NAUI going to rake you over the coals for this one." Pete began pulling out the tanks from the stern of the *Vagabond*. "Where'd you go diving? Next to Painted Cave?"

Mike nodded. "Yeah, there's a cave off it. Great for bug hunting. Only it's got some back action."

"Why didn't you call the Coast Guard?"

Mike waved his hand. "I did. But, they're too far away. They'd take hours to get here. Hey, we can handle it, no problem."

"Yeah." Looking a little worried, Pete glanced at Buck.

"You have any idea where she is?"

"Yeah," Buck nodded. "I left a trail. A couple of Cathy's gloves, a tank, my orange bug bag. Maybe one of us can find the trail, if the silt hasn't covered it up. She's using her flashlight as a signal."

"Great. Okay, guys, how about giving me a hand with these tanks?" Pete handed one to Mike; then gave the other one to Buck. "Hey, Doc, what happened to you? You look a little green, man."

Buck shook his head. "I'm okay, Pete. Just a little short of breath." He put one of the tanks on the *Trident* and started back to get the other.

"He ran out of air surfacing," Mike explained, putting another cylinder down on the *Trident*.

"You gonna be okay to dive?" Pete glanced at Buck.

"Sure," Buck said. He pointed to six tanks that had been transferred to the *Trident*. "I figure we've each got a couple of hours of air."

Pete nodded at Mike. "We'd better take some line this time."

Mike frowned. "Matter of fact, I ran some down into the chamber already. But we could use some extra. How much have you got?"

Pete opened the gear box. "I've got about 600 feet."

"That'll work," Buck said, grabbing the line from Pete. "We can cut it in half." He began to measure it out.

Buck turned to Pete. "It's a good thing you know the configuration of this cave, buddy. It's a maze in there."

Pete lowered his eyes. "Well, to tell you the truth, Doc, I've never dived that cave."

"But you said you had at the marina," Buck protested. "I heard you..."

"Well, that was just in front of the girls." Pete didn't look Buck in the eye.

"Oh shit!" Buck slapped his fist against the boat. He should have known it. Pete was a braggart, especially when women were involved. Dismayed, Buck shook his head.

"So how are we going to do this, guys?" Pete asked, ignoring Buck's reaction as he stepped aboard the *Trident*.

Buck slackened the line to the *Vagabond* to keep the two boats from smacking against each other in the swells. The *Vagabond* drifted several feet away from the *Trident*.

Buck reflected. "Since I'm the one who left the trail, I think I should go back in there. Especially since Mike's been having trouble with his vertigo."

"Sounds reasonable."

Mike shrugged. "It's up to you, Doc."

Buck nodded. "Pete, why don't you and I head back in the tunnels? We can each take separate directions. Mike can stay at the entrance. We'll each run a line back. If either of us feels like we're on the right trail, we can just tug on the line, and Mike can bring in the extra tank for Cathy."

"Okay," Pete agreed. "Three tugs, then a pause, then another three tugs will mean one of us has found the trail."

"Good," Buck said. "Mike can keep a spare tank at the tunnel and we'll each take one in with us."

"Gotcha." Mike nodded. He gave Buck a high five.

Pete folded his arms. "Okay, how about giving me the layout of this cave, guys."

Buck nodded. "Okay, this is it. It's kidney shaped. There's a tunnel in the back on the far left of the chamber. That's where we originally got lost. Then there are numerous tunnels and cracks leading off of that tunnel. Which one she's in, I don't know."

"How far back do you think she is?"

"I'd say about 250 feet," Buck reflected. "Maybe a little more." He looked at Mike stashing his knife in the sheath on his leg. "Is your dive knife sharp?"

"Like a razor," Mike responded.

"Great," Buck said. "Well, let's get going. I figure we've got about a hour and a half of bottom time with the extra tanks. That's ten minutes down and some extra time in case of an emergency. Mike ran a line down earlier and took an extra tank. That means we stay in the tunnel no more than an hour and a half max, agreed?"

Mike gave him a punch in the elbow. "Let's do it, Doc."

"How's the surge?" Pete asked.

Buck wrinkled his brow. "It's picking up."

"That figures," Pete frowned. "It's always worse in the afternoon. It can lay the kelp flat. Diving in it is a real bitch." He strapped on his BC.

"Why don't we follow the anchor line down, guys," Mike suggested. "I tied a line from it to the cave."

Pete nodded. "Okay, that's probably the best way down."

"Let's try not to stir up that silt," Buck said. "Vis is already bad."

Pete put on his mask. "Will do."

Buck zipped up his wet suit. "Any other thoughts before we get started?"

Pete shook his head. "Nope. How about we put this thing into action?"

"I'm with you." Buck shoved his mask on his face.

Pete zipped up his suit and grabbed one of the tanks. "There's sharks around here and the surge is bad, take it from me. The caves out here give me the willies." Pete looked a little nervous.

"You gonna be okay down there?" Buck asked.

"Oh, sure," Pete said nonchalantly. "No problem."

Buck glanced at his buddy. He had the feeling Pete was a lot more scared than he was making out.

"I don't like this whole thing," Lynn interrupted. "Suppose something happens down there. Suppose one of you gets hurt."

"Lynn, would you stop worrying about everything?" Buck snapped. "Just relax." Jesus! He was starting to get really irritated with her.

Lynn gasped. "Oh, my God, I think I saw a shark fin!"

Buck stared off into the distance. She was right. He saw the dorsal fin of a blue. Later in the afternoon, there'd probably be more in the vicinity. "It was just a blue," Buck said, reassuring her. "They've been swimming around here all day. They don't start biting until the evening."

Lynn pursed her lips. "Well, let's hope they don't feel like a little snack before dinner."

Buck wasn't worried about the sharks, although Pete was right about the surge. It could present problems until they got to the cave. It was probably running strong.

They all slipped into the rest of their gear, grabbed extra tanks, strapped them to their sides, and waddled in their fins to the dive ladder.

Anxious, Lynn followed them to the stern. "I hope you guys are going to be okay."

"Honey, we'll be fine." Buck pulled her toward him and gave her a light kiss on the head. "These guys are the best in the business. I can't think of anyone I'd be safer with, can you?"

She frowned, pulled away from him and turned to face the ocean. He couldn't see the expression on her face.

CHAPTER

15

MIKE SPLASHED DOWN INTO the water, followed by Buck and then Pete. The three grabbed the anchor line and began to descend toward the bottom.

The sea conditions had changed considerably since the morning. Twisting and torquing because of the strong surge action, the golden brown blades of kelp looked like a jungle in the middle of a gale.

As they approached the island wall, the surge was even stronger. It coincided with the swells above, coming in sets, separated by periods of relative calm. When a large swell rolled in, it kicked up vegetation and pieces of small shells from the bottom, scattering them everywhere.

Before he had time to cover his face with his arms, Mike was hit in the cheek by the sharp spines of a sea urchin. He felt like he was on patrol in Vietnam during the monsoon season with nipa palms whirling around in all directions, slapping against the men's faces and thighs.

He remembered Vietnam — shots coming from all directions, ripping through the watery jungle and pieces of bark scattering around him. The VC were nowhere in sight, but he knew they were out there. He felt uneasy, wondering whether a grenade was going to explode near him. Every crack of lightning from the storm made him jittery and he was running with all his might.

Mike's mind returned to the present. He thought he'd never have to return to this hell hole. Instead, he was confronting it head on.

As the divers swam closer to the island wall, a sickening feeling began to build in Mike's stomach. It was only a matter of time before they reached the cave. He knew something had to be done to stop this rescue mission. But what? He couldn't let Buck or Pete find Cathy. She couldn't come out alive.

The divers descended to the bottom of the anchor line. In a moment, they located the jagged rock where Mike had tied his line. Buck yanked on it and the three of them proceeded forward, using the rope to steady themselves against the force of the surge.

With the help of the line, they approached the cave without being smacked into the island walls. Mike took one look at the yawning gap, now reminding him of a devilish malignant grin, and as he crossed over the threshold, he felt a sickening dread.

Inside, the sandy bottom was rippled with deep crevices from the force of the surge. Even though the light was dimmed, they could see.

When they all got to the tunnel entrance, they spotted the tank Mike had brought down earlier. In a moment, Buck and Pete began to tie their lines to Mike's weight belt.

As Buck and Pete occupied themselves with the lines, Mike used the time to think. He hadn't called the Coast

Guard about the incident, even though he'd told Buck and Pete he had, so he didn't have to worry about their interference. Yet, there was the very real possibility that Buck or Pete might locate the trail and he'd have to get rid of one of them.

But there was no urgency unless it looked like they were on the right track. He'd wait this one out — see if they located the trail.

What could he do? He couldn't arouse suspicion. It would have to look like an accident. He thought of various alternatives. He could cut the line, but it would be a clean cut. The police would suspect foul play and Buck or Pete might find their way back.

Maybe one of them could drown in this cave. But how? Could he close off the valve on either of their tanks, sealing off the air supply? That just might work.

He had the element of surprise. He could use it to his advantage. Mike was highly trained in the art of killing. Nobody could be as deadly underwater.

Quickly, his mind choreographed the impending scene. He would wait for a tug on the line. That would mean Buck or Pete had almost found Cathy. Then it was Mike's job to bring the tank in for the rescue.

Only there would be no rescue. Instead, he would locate the diver, knock him out with the tank and close off the air valve located on his back below his neck.

Even if Buck or Pete were conscious, it would be hard to reach that valve. Instantly, the diver would be out of air. In less than a minute, he would drown. Then Mike could bleed the tank.

If the body was found, there would be no evidence of any wrongdoing. It would look like the diver had run out of air.

As Mike finished formulating his plan, Buck and Pete

made their way into the tunnel. Mike switched on his dive light and shone it into the tunnel entrance, but it was still too silty to see more than five feet in front of him. Good. The less visibility, the better.

Mike watched Buck and Pete as they moved forward, inch by inch. Mike held onto both lines, so he could feel if one of the divers gave the signal. He watched the black open gullet gulp them down, until he saw nothing but a wavering flipper disappearing into the darkness.

Mike waited an endless thirty minutes. He turned on his flashlight and glanced at his pressure gauge. He'd used up a lot of his air. He hoped that Buck or Pete would get low on air before they found the trail. Then they would have to turn around and come back. The rescue attempt could be aborted and by that time, it might be too late.

Mike pondered the probability of either Pete or Buck finding Cathy. Actually, the chances were not so good. They couldn't rely on direction. The cave was an amorphous mass of tunnels and crevices. They couldn't rely on visibility. The silt had covered everything like a black veil, and even with a flashlight, things were still opaque.

The divers could only rely on the markers Buck had left earlier, and the only way to find those was to feel their way along the tunnel's bottom, stirring up even more silt and making visibility even worse. So, all was not lost.

Oh shit! A sudden tug on the line brought him back to the present. It was from Buck. Two more tugs. Then a pause. Then three more tugs. Buck had found the right trail. Mike had no choice. He had to act. He had to kill Buck.

Knowing that this was a race against time, Mike quickly untied the line at his weight belt and knotted it around a rock. He snatched up the spare tank and started into the tunnel.

He had to stop the Doc before he reached Cathy; but he knew he had a better chance of finding Buck than Buck had of finding the next marker. Mike already had a pathway — the line. Buck had to slowly feel his way along the cave bottom, groping for his markers.

Mike stealthily reached for the line, and half swam, half dragged himself forward. The flashlight was of little help, although he kept it on.

Once he was deep inside the tunnel, he felt something sweep by his face. He reached out and grabbed a fin and then a leg. Aha! He'd found Buck. There was no time to waste.

He chucked his light on his side. He took a deep breath. With the added buoyancy, his body rose up a foot. He waited...one second, then two.

Quickly, when Buck was below him, he made a drastic move and caught the Doc entirely by surprise. With one powerful movement, he hurled the heavy cylinder down on Buck's head.

The impact of the blow was enough to stun Buck. He went limp. The spare tank rolled off his back and sank into the sludge below, sending up a burst of black silt.

It was just the chance Mike needed. He mounted Buck, held him in a leg lock, reached out and grasped his valve. In a flash, he twisted the valve to the right four times, cutting off the air supply entirely.

But, what was happening? The blow should have knocked Buck out cold. Instead, the Doc was moving.

Oh, hell! Mike should have realized that the impact of the blow would be lessened underwater. Buck was still conscious and now he was groping behind his neck with his right arm.

Buck struggled frantically, grasping for the valve to switch it on.

Instantly, Mike blocked Buck's reach, grabbing his arm.

Trying to free himself from Mike's deadly hold, Buck writhed in the water.

The silt rose up like a gigantic black boa constrictor, twisting its way to the ceiling and engulfing them both.

Aware of imminent disaster, Buck struggled instinctively, rolling on his side and taking Mike down with him.

Mike felt himself falling, down, down, down to the murky bottom, into the seething silt. He was shoved backwards by a powerful thrust of Buck's body. His shoulder pounded against the jagged rocky wall. Waves of white hot pain shot through his arm.

Mike held on, tackling Buck and still managing to keep his leg lock despite the lancing pain down his shoulder.

But, wait. Something just...wasn't right. Buck should be growing weaker with the lack of air. Instead, he was gaining strength and putting up a damned good fight. What the hell was going on?

Panicking, Mike breathed hard on his regulator. There was no way Buck could be alive...unless... That was it! Buck was breathing off the spare tank. Hell, Buck was no dummy. He had immediately gone for an alternate supply of air. It was the only way he could be still breathing.

Spontaneously, Mike went for Buck's mask, ripping it off his face. Then with his left arm, he grabbed Buck around his neck. He pulled back as tight as he could, trying to force the air from Buck's lungs.

But Buck rebounded, shoving Mike against the rocks on the side of the cave. A cascade of rubble tumbled from the wall, hitting Mike's mask.

The blow left Mike dazed. He hesitated in drawing from his regulator.

The momentary pause gave Buck the opportunity he needed. Mike felt a powerful jab in his ribs. The pain shot up his body in throbbing bursts. Goddamn! Buck had struck him with his elbow. Mike was forced to loosen his grip.

That was all Buck needed to gain time for an assault. Instantly, Buck reached back and ripped out Mike's regulator.

Then Mike felt a sharp stabbing pain in his left shoulder. His grip on Buck weakened. He felt Buck's body jerk away. A fin slapped his face.

He reached up and felt his own wet suit. There was a knife in his arm. Hell, he was cut! Buck had swiftly gone for his dive knife and plunged the blade into his shoulder!

Shit, his strength was subsiding. His body was going limp. He groped for his regulator and finding it, took a big draw of precious air.

He crawled to the wall and propped himself up against the cave. He yanked the knife from his shoulder. The pain was excruciating.

He grabbed his light and swept the beam around him, but he couldn't see a thing. He felt like he was in some sort of a black snowstorm with minute flakes whirling around him. He had to find Buck and stop him. He breathed hard on his regulator, the bubbles roaring in his ears.

Damn! Buck had vanished into the labyrinth.

CHAPTER

16

GOD!...NO...WHAT?...WHAT was going on?

Trying to get away from Mike's grasp, Buck scrambled up from the twisted bowels of the cave floor. The tunnel was pitch black. Mike...Mike...had tried to kill him! Mike, his buddy! Mike had cut off his air!

He had to get away. He had to get out of this hell hole. He had to get away NOW!

He spun around, flicking up mounds of silt and kicking furiously. If he didn't get away instantly, Mike would attack again. That flesh wound from the knife wouldn't deter him. In no time, he would recover. He'd come at Buck again, and this time, Mike was the only one with a weapon.

Mike was ingeniously adroit when it came to the deadly arts. Buck did not want to tackle a Navy SEAL underwater.

But which way to go? He was as good as dead if he couldn't find a way out.

Buck realized the only way out was to follow the line.

Quickly untying the line from his weight belt, he probed along the jagged wall until he found a ledge. He wrapped the cord around it, then tied it with a knot. He yanked at the line. It was taut — tight as a steel guitar string.

Swimming as fast as he could, he started out at a reckless speed. His heart tripped frantically against his rib cage. The blood vessels tightened in his head. He breathed hard on the regulator, his lungs taking in increasing gulps of air. He needed all the air he could get to keep up this pace, even though it was valuable.

Buck suspected that Mike was recovering from his stab wound and feeling his way along the jagged walls for Buck's line. It wouldn't take long to find it. Mike would be right behind Buck.

Tugging at the line, Buck raced through the black silty water. He kicked his legs like crazy.

When he had gone only a short way, he felt a yank on the line. Shit! There was no time to waste. Mike was already hot on his trail.

Even though his legs ached, Buck kicked even harder.

After what seemed like an eternity, he approached the opening to the chamber. He bolted forward and followed the line along the chamber wall.

He swam quickly to the jagged rock where Mike had tied the line. Desperately, he pulled at it until he found the knot and tried to untie it.

The line was Mike's pathway out of the cave. But the line stubbornly resisted all his manipulations. Hell! He could have cut it, but Mike had his knife.

Quickly, he abandoned the knot. He had no choice. If he waited much longer, Mike would be out of the cave.

He made his way along the chamber until he saw the circle of light that meant open water. He flew out of the cave and into the ocean, swimming frantically toward the anchor line.

Although Mike was a better swimmer, he was wounded, and that would give Buck a good head start. If he could make it to the boat, he could radio the Coast Guard.

Buck knew Mike kept a gun on board the _Trident_ in case of an emergency. It was in the storage compartment in the lower helm under the wheel. He had a chance of holding Mike off with the gun.

Buck followed the anchor line through the kelp forest, northwest to the _Trident_. Once he began his ascent, he slowed down, even though he wanted desperately to speed ahead.

Finally, when he spotted the hull rocking back and forth in the troughs, he knew he was close. Only ten more yards! Five! Then one!

He saw the dive ladder just ahead. With a sudden burst of speed, he popped out of the water like a cork out of a champagne bottle.

He grabbed the dive rail and heaved himself up to the deck. "Lynn," he yelled. "Lynn, get over here quick!"

Lynn was reading a magazine. Instantly, she threw it down, leapt from her chair and started for the dive ladder. "What's going on? Did you find Cathy?"

Buck shook his head. "No. Help me out of this gear quickly, honey." He pulled off his flippers.

"Where's Mike and Pete?" she asked, unsnapping his BC.

"I don't know."

"You don't know? What happened?"

He chucked his mask and flippers and stripped off his BC. "Look, Lynn, Mike tried to cut off my air."

Her eyes opened wide. "He did what?"

"He tried to kill me. Look, I can't handle this on my

own. We've got to radio the Coast Guard."

He stood up, unzipped his suit and sprinted to the salon door. He yanked it open. The door slammed against the side of the *Trident* with a bang.

Lynn ran after him.

He charged for the control panel at the helm.

"Where is Mike?" she repeated.

"In the cave. I stabbed him with my dive knife."

"Oh, my God!"

He whirled around to face her. "It was the only way. He's not dead. It was just a flesh wound." He grabbed her by the shoulders. "Look, hon, I don't have time to explain. I've got to radio the Coast Guard. I don't think he ever notified them." He paused. "Can you help me?"

"What do you want me to do?" She looked terrified.

He grabbed the mike from the control panel. "There's a gun under the storage cabinet," he said, pointing below him. "Get it out, will you? We're going to need it." He dropped down in front of the control panel.

"Here?" she asked, kneeling down at his feet.

"Yeah."

She retrieved a black box, opened it and grabbed the steel handle of a .45 automatic.

"That's it. Just hold onto it." He quickly reached over to the control panel, punched up the distress channel 16 on the radio keypad and keyed the mike. "Mayday, mayday. This is *Trident*, located in a cove just west of Painted Cave. *Trident* is a thirty-five foot sports fisher, white hull, blue trim. Urgent. This is Buck Connors. Over."

Lynn's lips were trembling. She looked as if she were about to cry.

"Don't worry, hon," he said, trying to calm her down. "Everything will be all right."

He heard the sound of footsteps across the deck of the

Trident. The salon door smacked open.

Holding the gun in both her hands, Lynn whirled around and pointed the barrel in the direction of the noise.

"*Trident,* this is the Coast Guard Station, Channel Islands. Received mayday..."

"Put down that mike."

It was Mike's voice.

Buck felt a chill go up his spine.

Quickly, Buck turned around to see Mike standing directly behind him. His shoulder was tied with a rag and his arm was bloody. He was holding his wounded arm in his hand.

Lynn rushed over to him. "Mike!" she shouted. "Are you all right?"

"I'm fine," he responded. "It's your husband that's in trouble." He faced Buck. "Put down that mike, buddy." Mike spat out the words.

Buck was furious. "Don't call me that. I'm not your buddy. You tried to kill me, you bastard."

"*Trident, Trident,* this is the Coast Guard, Channel Islands...." came the voice over the speaker.

"Hold on, Channel Islands...," Buck said.

Buck turned to his wife. "Give me the gun, Lynn."

Lynn flipped around. She pointed the gun directly at Buck's chest.

"Lynn!" Buck shouted. "What are you doing? This son-of-a-bitch tried to kill me. Give me the gun."

Mike stepped forward and yanked the mike out of Buck's hands. "That wasn't too smart, asshole." He turned off the radio.

"Lynn, give me the gun!" Buck yelled.

Lynn handed the gun to Mike.

Buck glanced at Lynn and Mike standing together.

Lynn put her arms around Mike's waist and hugged

him.

Buck's mouth opened in surprise.

His head reeled. Down in that cave, he'd been wondering how she would support herself once he was gone, while up above, she'd only been concerned for Mike.

Buck turned away from the two in disgust.

His perfect life had been a fake. He'd always believed he had a happy family and a pretty good marriage, at least as good as the next guy's. Why hadn't he realized that all those nights when she went out, leaving him alone with the kids, that she had cared nothing for them?

Hell, she'd been out screwing his dive buddy.

He felt like his chest was going to explode with agony. He could hardly breathe.

He'd been a fool. He'd seen the signs – her nights out with the girls, the new wardrobe. He'd felt her coldness.

But, he'd denied his feelings, pretended everything was fine, because all he'd ever wanted was an ordinary life. He didn't want his kids to go through what he had gone through as a child. More than anything, he didn't want to break up his family.

Buck's fists tightened into a ball and he whirled around to face Lynn. "You bitch!" he shouted, pointing his finger at Lynn.

"Hey, that's no way to talk to your wife," Mike interjected.

Buck shook his head. "She's no wife of mine."

"Right-o, Doc. After today, she'll be a widow."

Oh, Lord, thought Buck. Mike was going to kill him.

Mike grinned deviously. "She looks great in black. Remember that low-cut evening dress she wore to the Christmas ball at the club? She was a knockout then, wasn't she, Buck?"

"Screw you, Mike."

Mike laughed. "Oh, not until you shower and shave, Doc."

Buck gritted his teeth.

Mike smiled. "I'm going to save your wife from a nasty divorce."

"Mike, you can't kill Buck!" Lynn shouted.

"Just watch me." Mike pointed the gun at Buck's chest.

Buck turned to Mike. "You left Cathy down in that cave to die. Now you're going to kill me. Don't you think the police are going to suspect?"

Lynn turned to Mike. "Buck is right. What if the police suspect?"

"The police are going to suspect nothing, Lynn, as long as you can keep your mouth shut and do as I say."

Lynn folded her arms coldly across her chest. "I'm just as innocent bystander in all this. I didn't leave Cathy in the cave."

Mike shook his head negatively. "Ah, Lynn, my dear, you're as involved in it as I am. Didn't we plan this together?"

"Plan it? I didn't plan it," she shouted.

"Weren't you the one who wished Cathy dead?" Mike argued. "All I did was what you wanted."

"You helped him plan this, Lynn?" Buck shouted. "How could you?"

"I didn't think he'd really do it... I didn't think he'd hurt you, Buck!" Lynn cried.

"Well, guess what, he has! You're a stupid bitch!"

Lynn opened her mouth in surprise. "Buck!"

Buck turned to Mike. "They're going to get your ass for this. They'll lock you up for good. This is murder."

Buck heard a banging noise from the stern.

"Hey, what the hell is going on?" Pete's voice yelled.

Mike jabbed the gun barrel in Buck's back. "Move it, Buck," he said, motioning for him to walk to the stern.

They found Pete on the deck of the boat near the dive step, shedding his gear. He stood up and walked toward them.

"What the fuck are you two doing, leaving me in that cave?" Pete said. He glared at Buck and Mike. "You want to get me killed?"

"Look out, Pete!" Buck shouted. "Mike's got a gun!"

Instantly, Buck ducked and then lunged at Mike and grabbed the gun. He slammed Mike's arm against the bulkhead and tackled him to the deck, trying to wrest the gun from him.

But Mike stubbornly held on, pointing the gun at Pete.

Buck saw Mike's finger press down on the trigger. "Noooo—" he shouted.

It was too late. He heard it — the sudden crack of bullets spraying the deck. The last hit Pete directly in the neck. Oh, shit!!!

A bloodcurdling scream ripped through the air.

Pete's body was thrown backwards. He fell overboard with a loud splash.

Almost instantly, Buck jerked his head around to see Lynn's mouth stretched into a horrified O.

"Oh, shit, Mike!" Buck yelled in shock. "You've killed Pete."

"Get up!" exclaimed Mike, recovering from the fight and gaining control of the gun. He grimaced in pain as he held his arm. Then he pulled himself up. "Get going!" He shoved Buck toward the cockpit gunnel.

"Oh, my God!" Lynn shrieked.

Pete's body lay face-up floating on the water. He was dead. His neck was almost completely severed at the jugular vein. Streaks of blood gushed into the water. Already, the water around Pete's body was beginning to turn a sickly dull red.

"Goddamn, look what you've done!" Buck yelled.

"It's your fault, Doc." Mike's mouth twisted into a contortion. "You're the one who jumped me."

"You're the one who fired the shots! You go to hell, you bastard! "

"Well, I think you're going there first." Mike raised the gun barrel to Buck's head.

Buck glared at Mike. "You sorry bastard. Pete's body is enough evidence to send you to prison for life. And you, too, Lynn. You're an accomplice! You're gonna spend your life behind bars."

"Oh, God!" Lynn shouted. "This is too much! I can't be part of this." She buried her head in her hands. "There's no way you can cover up Pete's murder."

"You're panicking, Lynn," Mike said. "Calm down. The sharks will smell the blood. It's almost feeding time. They'll finish him off."

Oh, damn! Buck thought, perusing Pete's body. Mike was right. The body was good shark bait. Mike could cover up his crime by feeding Pete to the sharks.

Mike nodded at Buck. "Yes, you just wait. In another half hour, there'll be swarms of sharks in this water."

Buck thought for a moment. Sharks didn't like the taste of human flesh. But they had poor eyesight. Anything bleeding or thrashing in the water attracted their attention. They thought it was a baby seal or a large fish in distress. So, they attacked. Their teeth were so sharp, they ripped through flesh, taking off an arm or a leg in no time. When they found out the flesh was human, they just spat it out.

He directed his attention toward the ocean. Out of the corner of his eye, Buck saw an ominous fin coming closer to the stern. All the noise must have attracted it.

He looked closer. Instinctively, he knew this shark wasn't one of the harmless blues. It wasn't circling. Instead, it cut straight through the waves. It was humongous — a good twenty feet long and probably 4,000 pounds. It must be a great white! It was so big, it could swallow Pete whole.

The shark moved steadily through the water and disappeared under the surface. Buck figured the shark was still there, searching stealthily for its prey.

A top level predator in open water, the great white used surprise and speed to attack its victim. Almost no one saw the monster coming. When it was ready to ambush, the attack was swift and deadly with no preliminary passes.

A great white's jaws were like a meat cleaver — clean, swift and sharp. Buck had seen a great white approach a baby seal in a matter of seconds and dice the head off cleaner than the scalpels in his office.

The fin reappeared on the surface. The shark was closing in on Pete's body, attracted by the blood. The fin vanished again.

Buck's eyes swept the water; then turned to Lynn. Her eyes were fixed on the ocean.

Buck's eyes followed her line of vision. Suddenly, he heard a loud rush of water and a crash as a heavy object broke the surface.

Lynn screamed.

The shark reared its ugly snout out of the water. The white underbelly of the animal rose above the surface. The gigantic maw opened, exposing pink flesh surrounding rows of razor-sharp teeth. In a flash, the monstrous jaws ripped into Pete's waist. Then it dragged the corpse underwater.

Buck gasped. In a moment, a leg, severed at the thigh, bobbed to the surface. He could see the bone protruding out of the torn bloody flesh.

Buck felt his stomach turn over. He retched violently.

He turned back to the ocean, looking for the rest of Pete's body, but nothing remained – only a surface whirlpool churning on the water.

CHAPTER

17

ON AND OFF, ON and off. Cathy didn't know how long she had been flashing this light. She had completely lost track of the time. She had stopped counting.

Irritated, she cut off the light. What good had it done? No one had come to her rescue.

She rubbed her hand across her brow. She was feeling *sooooo* sleepy.

She put her hand into the water and splashed some on her face. The cold water woke her up. She could slip down into the water and stay awake. Just use her BC to float. It was a tempting thought. Buck had done it earlier. No, better not, she thought. At least if she lost consciousness above water, she wouldn't drown.

The neoprene wet suit was beginning to feel stiff and confining. It especially felt tight around her arms. She took her knife and cut the seam up to her elbows and from her ankles to her knees. That was better. At least she didn't feel as if she was wrapped like a mummy.

At the moment, all she really wanted to do was go to

sleep. But that would seal her fate. How would anyone find her in all these crevices without the flashlight blinking on and off? All the nooks and crannies in this cave looked the same. She had to stay awake at all costs.

She turned the flashlight on again. On and off, on and off. What was that in the distance? A faint glow? Yes, and there was Mike at her side. They were at the Santa Barbara Marina. It was night.

She watched the distant lights on the boats bobbing with the waves. "It's so beautiful out here."

She felt comfortable and warm and loved. He was holding her against his strong chest. A cold drift of ocean wind blew against her hair. She brushed it back from her face. "I wish we could be like this forever," she said dreamily.

"We can." He reached into his pocket, took out a small blue velvet box and opened it. Inside was a beautiful tear-shaped diamond engagement ring. "Cathy," he said, slipping the ring on her finger. "I want to marry you."

She held her finger up and admired the scintillating light reflecting off the many facets. "It's the most beautiful ring I've ever seen, Mike. Of course, I'll marry you."

He smiled. He leaned toward her and put his arms around her shoulders. He bent down and kissed her gently on her lips. On her hand, the ring twinkled on and off, on and off.

His lips took her breath away, sucked the breath into his. With each kiss, her breath seemed to be vanishing.

She tried to push him away. She couldn't breathe. She tried to say something, but her lips stopped her from speaking. She pushed and pushed, but he gripped her strongly around the waist.

The ring danced in the light like the effects of a psychedelic drug. On and off, on and off.

I can't breathe, I can't breathe, she thought over and over to herself.

A soft plop in the water roused her from sort of a half sleep. She'd been hallucinating. Was someone else in this cave?

"Hello," she yelled. "Hello, I'm over here. Mike, Buck, I'm here."

"Here, here, here." The words reverberated through the chamber as if mocking her.

She tightened her hand, but felt a sensation of emptiness in her balled fists. The flashlight! It wasn't there. In her sleep, she must have nudged it and knocked it into the water. Damn! That must have been the sound she'd heard.

She felt her body stiffen in sudden panic. She had to find the flashlight! Where was it?

She thought for a moment. If the flashlight had fallen out of her hands, it would have gone straight down to the bottom. There was no current, so it couldn't be very far.

She had to dive down and get it. But, whatever she did, she couldn't afford to be swimming around all over this cavern searching for that flashlight. She'd get lost, and she'd never find this air pocket again. She'd be as good as dead if she strayed too far from the ledge.

She gritted her teeth, took a deep breath and forced herself to jump off the ledge into the murky water.

Her hands sank wrist deep into the silt as she felt blindly along the muddy bottom. She felt something hard. She ran her fingertips over it. It was Buck's lobster bag.

Disappointed, she pulled her hand away and searched farther away from the spot. Her lungs were beginning to burn now. She would need to resurface soon.

Finally, she felt the hard cylindrical shape of the dive

light. Relieved, she grabbed it and headed straight up. She broke the surface, took a breath of the noxious air and coughed.

Dripping with water, she climbed back up on the ledge. Trembling, she turned the flashlight on again. Thank God. Nothing damaged. It worked fine. She began to flash it again, on and off, on and off.

Suddenly, for no reason at all, except from relief or fear, she burst into tears. What if she hadn't found the light? What then? Would she have been sealed in this dark crypt?

She put her arms around her shoulders, rocked herself and tried to calm down. Finally, her sobbing ceased. She felt tired again. Her breathing was growing more rapid, a marked sign of CO_2 buildup. She wouldn't last much longer.

She was so, so tired. What would it be like to be die here? She'd be buried alive.

She remembered going on a trip to Egypt once with Mike. They decided to visit the Pyramids in Giza. They walked around for awhile, then an Arab stopped them and asked if they'd like to see inside. It was noon and terribly hot.

"Sure," Mike said.

She was usually game. But the Arab looked shifty, glancing at them out of the corner of his eyes. He was a hunchback, dressed in long robes, and he was small and wrinkled. He used a staff to steady his walk as he led them inside.

Immediately, she felt she should never have come. The air was stale. It was dark, despite the Arab's lantern, and much too hot. The guide led them up a long narrow passageway of stairs hardly large enough for a human body to stand. At the top of the stairs, she wanted to go back, but Mike was still enthusiastic. He was always enthusiastic about everything. Why did he always have to take so many risks? He wasn't afraid of anything.

But she was afraid. What if the lantern went out? Or what if the guide had other designs? He could put out the light, rob them and leave them alone in the pyramid. They could die, if only from the heat. She'd heard of worse things happening in Cairo.

They finally reached the main chamber. Hieroglyphics along the walls. Pictures of people in angled poses. Pictures of those horrible beetles. What did they call them? Scarabs. Ugly bugs.

In the center of the room was a large crypt, supposedly once holding a mummy, a king, who had been wrapped in a shroud. Below, the Arab explained, all the king's servants and horses and wives had been buried. There was even a boat with paddles for the servants to steer them down a river to a nether world.

The guide explained that the servants had been buried alive. She supposed they just ran out of air in the pyramid while waiting to follow their king into a land beyond.

She imagined herself as one of those servants floating down a canal of darkness, floating, floating toward another kingdom, far from here. On and off, on and off. Beyond time and the sun. On and off, on and off. Drifting down a dark, dark passageway into a bottomless cavern, down to a sunless sea.

She was drifting, drifting into another world, through dark passageways, rowing down a river, rowing with dozens of other slaves, all skeletons, all dead.

But there was a light at the end of the tunnel, just up ahead, flashing on and off, on and off. She reached for the light, but it was growing dimmer and dimmer. She rowed harder, but it exceeded her grasp. She could never quite make it to the light.

She felt something cold brush against her leg. She opened her eyes wide with a start. She'd been dozing or perhaps hallucinating. At any rate, she'd been losing consciousness again. She suddenly realized the light from the flashlight was growing dimmer.

Damn! She rapped the light on the rock, and it grew brighter again, then started once more to fade. Oh, God! The battery was going dead. They'd never find her without the light. She was trapped in this watery crypt forever. Her fate was sealed.

Edgar Allan Poe had been her favorite writer when she was a child. Odd, that she should suffer the same fate as his heroines.

"The Black Cat." A cat walled inside a brick tomb with his mistress. The sound of its still-beating heart drives the murderer mad. "The Fall of the House of Usher." Madeline, buried alive, brings down her ancestral home. "Ligeia." Dying a premature death, she rises from the grave in the body of Rowena.

Would she be like all those Poe heroines, a victim of some freakish hand of fate, walled off in an underground tomb forever? Or would she come back from the dead, another Ligeia, to haunt those who had left her down here to die?

CHAPTER

18

B<small>UCK</small>, M<small>IKE AND</small> L<small>YNN</small> stood at the stern of the *Trident*. The water was streaked with Pete's blood and a foul stench of death filled the air.

Buck looked for a sign of the great white, but saw nothing, not even a fin. He suspected the shark was still swimming around the boat.

Mike raised the gun to Buck's head. He smiled. "I was right, wasn't I?"

Lynn bit her lips nervously. "This is too many murders, Mike. You'll never get away with it."

"I'll be fine, Lynn, just fine," Mike reassured her. "Now, that shark is probably looking for a second course. What do you think, Buck?"

"I think it may ignore me," Buck said. "Especially after it's had a bite of Pete."

Mike cocked the gun. "Oh, I doubt that, Buck. I'm going to take care of that."

With his other hand, Mike reached for his dive knife at his ankle. So, that was it. Mike planned to stab him and then push him off the boat. Once the shark sensed his thrashing and the extra blood, it would come directly for him.

"No!" Lynn shouted. In a flash, she raced toward Mike, grabbing his wrist and trying to wrest the gun from his grasp.

Buck ducked, trying to get out of the line of fire.

Shots blasted through the air, ripping through the deck.

Lynn struggled with Mike, but he regained control of the gun. He pushed her away.

"Goddamn, Lynn!" Mike yelled in rage, hurling the gun in the ocean. "Look what you've done! There are no more bullets!"

Buck sized up the situation. He didn't have the strength to fight off a Navy SEAL, especially one with a knife. But maybe, since Mike had a stab wound in his arm, Buck could get the upper hand.

He took the initiative, leaping toward Mike and taking a strong right jab to his jaw.

Mike reeled backwards, the side of his head hitting the stainless steel flybridge ladder. Dazed, he slumped down, the knife sliding out of his hand and clattering to the deck.

Instantly, Buck dropped to his knees and seized the knife.

Mike wiped his hand across his mouth. It was dripping with blood. He slowly got to his feet and lunged at Buck. His massive arms were like a battering ram.

The force flung Buck against the cockpit gunnel. Jesus! Flashes of pain leapt up his spine.

Avoiding the knife, Mike managed to grab Buck's wrists.

The two went nose-to-nose as Buck tried to push him away, but Mike was too strong. He shoved Buck's arm backwards, trying to force him to loosen his hold on the knife.

Buck refused to let go, even though he felt his strength draining from his body. His head dangled over the transom.

Now Mike took another tactic, twisting Buck's wrist so the knife blade was pointed at Buck's neck. Oh shit! Mike was trying to slash his jugular vein.

The knife inched closer.

Buck knew he couldn't hold Mike off forever. He had to use all his strength — NOW! He gave a last ditch effort — one mighty shove.

He felt Mike's hold loosen. Mike lost his balance and was hurled backwards, his head slamming against the salon bulkhead.

The sudden jolt knocked the knife out of Buck's hand. It dropped to the cap rail.

Mike lunged at the knife, trying to get to it, but Buck kicked it over the side. It splashed into the ocean.

Mike's chin hit the stern as he grappled for the knife, but it was too late.

Mike turned around, an angry grimace on his face. "You son of a bitch!" he shouted.

Quickly, Buck jumped on Mike, tackling him. He thrust Mike's elbows against the stern. Then he slammed him in the jaw with his fist.

The force of the blow smacked Mike's head backwards against the transom. His eyes rolled back in his head. He slumped down.

Buck stood with his fists in the air, ready for another blow, but Mike didn't retaliate. He lay still. Slowly, Buck let his arms fall to his side.

Mike's chest rose and fell. He was still alive, but Buck's last shot had knocked him unconscious.

Buck felt the world spinning around him. A whirlpool swelled in the pit of his stomach. Dizzy, he pushed against the bridge ladder, trying to regain his balance.

He put his hand to his head. He felt like a kid taking his first ride on a roller coaster. He leaned over the side of the boat and vomited. Then, he righted himself, wiped his hand across his mouth and glanced back at Mike.

Mike hadn't moved. But Lynn was crouching over him. "What have you done?" She took her lover's head in her hands and put it in her lap. "Have you killed him?"

"I wish I had," Buck balled his fists in anger. What a wife!

In disgust, he turned away. He gazed out at the horizon, trying to calm himself.

When he looked back, Lynn was seated in one of the deck chairs. She was rocking back and forth and crying softly.

He would have comforted her, if she had shown any feeling for anyone other than herself. But he felt nothing for her now but anger.

He rubbed his chin. Cathy was still trapped. His first mission was to get her out of that cave. Jeff and Judy and the three babes would be no help at all. He needed professionals for the job. He would put in another call to the Coast Guard.

Instantly, he headed toward the salon, passing Mike's slouched body. The asshole was still out cold, but Buck knew he had to act fast.

Buck opened the salon door, then slammed and locked it, in case Mike came around. He made his way to the lower helm and picked up the mike at the control panel.

Suddenly, his nostrils caught the faint whiff of a strange smell. What was that odor? He sniffed again. Gasoline fumes! Shit! The air was filling with gas vapor. The bullets must have punctured the fuel system.

He wiped his brow. Thank God, his sinuses had cleared up and he'd been able to smell! Otherwise, he might have started the engine and the entire boat could have exploded into flames.

If he wanted to get anywhere, to the other side of the island, or to Santa Barbara, he would have to use Jeff's motor yacht.

He kept his hands away from the ignition as he punched up the distress channel 16 on the radio again. He keyed the mike. "Mayday, mayday. This is *Trident*, located one cove west of Painted Cave on Santa Cruz Island. *Trident* is a thirty-five foot sports fisher, white hull, blue trim. Urgent. This is Buck Connors. Over."

He waited a moment. There was a crackle on the radio and a voice. "*Trident, Trident,* this is the Coast Guard Station, Channel Islands. We have been monitoring your radio conversations. We have a cutter in route with an estimated time of arrival of twenty minutes. Over."

Buck sighed in relief. He held up the mike. "You know we have a dive incident on board our boat?"

He heard some static on the mike. "Roger, *Trident*. What is the status of your diver? Over."

"She's trapped in an underground cave. "

"How much air supply does she have? Over."

"I don't know. I don't know the source of the air. Most likely, it's limited. She probably has several hours. "

"Have you made an attempt to rescue her? Over."

"Yes, but I failed." He paused. "Coast Guard, I have another situation on board. We've had an attempted murder by the owner of the boat — Mike Gallagher. I knocked him out, but I don't know for how long."

"Roger, stand by, Buck. I'll notify the *Blackfin* of your situation. Over."

There was a silence and crackle as Buck waited for the station to call the *Blackfin*. A moment later the Channel Islands Coast Guard station was back on the air. "*Trident*, we have apprised the *Blackfin* of your situation. Have you checked on the status of the owner of the boat? Is he still unconscious? Over."

"He was a few minutes ago."

"Does he look like is still breathing? Over."

"Yes, he's okay. I'm a doctor," replied Buck. "He's just unconscious."

"Okay, Buck, are you safe?"

"For the moment. As long as he doesn't come around, I'll be okay. "

"Have you restrained him? Over."

"I haven't had time."

"We suggest you restrain him. Do you have any line on board?"

"We used it all trying to rescue the diver. I'll try to find something else."

"Okay, Buck, hang tight. We're on our way. Over."

Buck sighed in relief. He put down the mike and glanced around the salon for some line.

Without warning, there was a crash. He whirled around to see Mike's fist smashing through the salon door window. Then Mike quickly unlatched the lock, thrust the door open and raced through the salon toward Buck.

Jesus! Buck looked around for a weapon — anything to protect himself. In a corner was a spear gun. He reached out and grabbed the gun. As Mike entered the helm, Buck slammed the metal side against Mike's head.

The spear gun dazed Mike momentarily, but he recovered and hurled himself forward, shoving Buck backwards against the side of the salon.

Buck slumped to the floor.

Mike stood over him, ready to hit again, but Buck thrust out his leg and kicked him in the face.

Buck had just enough time to crawl to the door. Quickly, he unlocked it, opened it and half crawling, half walking managed to struggle outside. He shoved his weight against the door, trying to keep it closed, but Mike rammed his heavy body against it.

The door flew open, sending Buck backwards. His head hit the stern of the boat.

Flashes of pain raced up his body. Before he could recover, Mike punched him in the stomach. Buck doubled over in pain. Then Mike slammed him in the jaw, thrusting him backwards again.

Buck felt himself being lifted, and then instantly, he was flung through the air, landing in the water with a loud splash.

Buck felt a sudden chill as he hit the cold water. Then he felt himself sinking down, down, down into the ocean. He opened his eyes. Golden brown leaves of kelp surrounded his body, clutching at him.

Something hard hit his back. He started and turned around. He came face-to-face with Pete's mangled, bloody body tangled in the kelp forest. A surge of water shoved it against him, the still attached arm grabbing his shoulder.

The sight of the body freaked him out.

Panicking, he kicked the body away. It loosened from the kelp, rising slowly to the surface. Buck kicked frantically upward, surfacing through trails of blood.

Pete's body floated up behind him.

Terrified, Buck swam away from it. The shark was probably still in the vicinity. Crazed with all this blood in the water, it would probably attack again. He didn't want to be near Pete's corpse when it returned.

He peered over the waves. Shit! There was the dorsal fin of the great white again! He had to get to the dive ladder before the shark got to him. He started swimming to the ladder.

Mike was waiting for him at the dive ladder. "Sorry, Doc." He had a wicked gleam in his eye. "We're not taking anyone on board."

As Buck put his hands on the rail, Mike kicked him in the face. Damn! He touched his face and felt blood. The blow sent him back into the water.

"So long, Doc." Mike laughed.

Buck's heart sank. He glanced at Jeff's motor yacht, but boarding it was a lost cause without the swim ladder attached.

Mike called to Lynn from the stern of the boat. "Go start the engine. The keys are in the bridge ignition. I've weighed anchor. Let's get out of here." He untied the lines to Pete's boat.

"What about Buck?" Lynn began. "There's a shark out there!"

"Lynn, it's either me or him," Mike yelled. "Make a decision. Hurry up!"

Buck watched Lynn hesitate, but finally she turned back to the flybridge. "Lynn!" he shouted frantically. "Don't do it. Don't start the engine!"

She didn't listen to him. She hurried up the steps to the bridge. Oh, no! Everything was going to blow!

"Don't let her do it, Mike!" Buck warned. "There's a gas leak in the engine room!"

Mike's eyes opened wide. "Lynn!" he yelled, turning toward the flybridge.

But it was too late. Suddenly, there was a white flash and a booming explosion. Planks and metal blew sky high.

The force of the explosion hurled Mike's body over-board. Buck swam away from the wreckage with all his might, but the force jarred him to the bone. The water around him rippled with the shock wave. He cringed as debris splashed down all around him.

The flybridge burst into flames. The hull was taking on water fast. Crackling and popping, fiberglass and wood caught fire.

Oh, God! Lynn! If the force of the explosion hadn't thrown Lynn from the boat, she was dead. He watched in amazement as the whole boat was engulfed.

A burning fuel slick spread over the water. Luckily, he was out of its path. But Jeff's boat wasn't. It caught fire and the flames began to spread.

He quickly swam away from the boat.

He searched for any signs of the remains of Mike or Lynn among the wreckage.

Several yards off, he spotted Lynn's body and swam toward her. She was floating on her stomach.

He managed to turn her over. Her face was scratched badly and there were bruises on her body. He felt her breath against his face. Miraculously, she was still alive! She moaned softly.

He grabbed a piece of floating debris in his left hand, and with the other arm, he held Lynn's head above the surface.

He scanned the horizon for Mike's body. He spotted him flailing in the water about ten yards away. Mike was bleeding from the knife wound and there were gashes on his face.

Buck glanced at the island. It was a long swim to shore. If Mike came at him again, he'd have to fight him off and let go of Lynn. In her dazed state, Lynn would probably drown. He no longer had any feelings for his wife, although he felt a certain obligation not to let her die.

Abruptly, he saw the shark fin appear on the surface, heading in Mike's direction. The fresh blood from Mike's arm must have attracted it.

Buck stared, frozen with terror. Already, he could see the snout of the shark on the surface; then the ugly head reared out of the water, jaws agape, serrated teeth like a hundred large knifes ready to sever flesh.

The shark lunged at Mike's body.

A death-defying look spread across Mike's face when he saw the animal. In seconds, there was a crack as bones and sinews snapped and the shark's jaw sank down on Mike's shoulder.

Mike thrashed for a moment in the water, even after his arm was severed. Taking the arm with it, the shark dove below the surface. True to form, Mike didn't utter a sound, although his face registered a look of silent agony. Blood spewed out of his torn shoulder.

Buck turned away from the scene in horror. All that remained of both boats was burning wreckage. Heavy fumes and smoke filled the air. A fireball rolled up from the fuel slick on the water.

Buck positioned Lynn underneath his forearm, and with his left arm, started swimming away from the boats.

Lynn moaned. She was coming to. "What's going on?" she asked.

"Everything's fine, Lynn," Buck said.

Yet he knew everything was far from fine.

He glanced at the water. He hadn't seen the shark again, but he knew it was lurking below the surface. The noise from the explosion might have scared it away, but only for the moment. It would return. It could attack Mike again or it could be right underneath him. Even if he tried to swim to shore, the noise would attract the animal. He had to get out of the water.

Goddamn, where was the Coast Guard?

CHAPTER

19

THE *BLACKFIN*, AN EIGHTY-SEVEN foot long Coast Guard cutter with bright orange-red and blue stripes across its beam and bow, was racing at her top speed of twenty-five knots in open water toward Santa Cruz Island. With her high rise superstructure, she had been built specifically for rescue operations.

Rigged to the side of the cutter was a smaller craft used for rescue and assistance — a rigid-hull inflatable Avon, built of fiberglass with rubber pontoons on the sides and equipped with a 150 horsepower outboard motor.

On board the cutter were Sergeant Rick Humphries and the four divers from the Ventura County Sheriff's Department — Johnny Bailey; Rex Simmons, a Camarillo landscaper; Ed Connolly, a patrol officer doubling as part of the dive team; and John Daniels, a retired naval officer.

While the dive team was getting outfitted, four Coast Guard members readied the rest of the equipment at the stern.

At the helm, Petty Officer First Class Brent Woodward scanned the horizon with his binoculars. Brilliant fiery rays from the setting sun streaked across the sky.

Woodward frowned and swept his hand in frustration through his sandy brown hair. There was no sign of the boat.

"See if you can see anything," he said, handing the binoculars to his assistant, Petty Officer Third Class Bill Watkins.

Watkins took the binoculars and scanned the horizon. He shook his head. "Negative." He handed the binoculars back to Woodward.

Woodward took another reading of his position and altered course. They should be nearly on top of the vessel. "Take another look, will you, Bill?"

Watkins peered through the binoculars. Suddenly, off on the horizon, he spotted a mass of billowing black smoke in the sky. "Damn, take a look at this."

Woodward grabbed the binoculars. He gazed through them. "Uh, oh. Better tell the lieutenant."

"Will do," Watkins said, immediately opening the door of the pilot house and hurrying out.

Lieutenant Junior Grade Edward Barnes was at the stern with members of his crew and the sheriff's department divers. He was conferring with Sergeant Humphries concerning the plans for the rescue when he was interrupted by Watkins.

"Lieutenant," Watkins said. "We've spotted a lot of smoke rising from the vessel in distress."

Lieutenant Barnes, who usually had a calm easygoing demeanor, raised his eyebrows in alarm. "I'd better take a look." He followed Watkins back into the pilot house.

Woodward handed Barnes the binoculars. "She's on the port side, sir."

"I see her. See if you can get her on the radio, Bill," he nodded to the Petty Officer. "Then notify the station."

"Will do, Lieutenant," Watkins said.

"Proceed full speed ahead. I'll notify the crew to break out the fire fighting equipment."

"Yes, sir," Woodward replied, as the lieutenant rushed out of the pilot house and to the stern.

Barnes immediately ordered the team to bring out canisters of PKP, a chemical to suffocate the fire, and standard CO_2 extinguishers. They also pulled out the fire hoses attached to pumps to suck up sea water.

Watkins punched up channel 16 on the radio console and keyed the mike. "*Trident, Trident,* this is the Coast Guard cutter *Blackfin.* Come in. Over."

There was no answer.

"Try it again," Woodward said.

"Roger," Watkins responded. "*Trident, Trident,* this is the Coast Guard cutter *Blackfin.* Do you read? Over."

There was still no answer.

"Try one more time, Watkins," Woodward said. "If they don't answer, put in a call to the station."

"*Trident,* this is the Coast Guard cutter *Blackfin.* Do you read? Over."

Still, there was no answer.

"All right," Woodward said. "Notify the station that we've lost contact with the vessel in distress."

Watkins nodded. He switched channels to the station at Channel Islands Harbor. "This is the *Blackfin.* We are in the vicinity of the *Trident.* We have visual contact. There's a lot of black smoke and it appears the vessel may have gone down. We've been unable to establish communication with her. Over."

"Do you see any survivors in the water? Over."

"Negative, Station. Stand by. "

As the cutter approached the burning vessel, the crew members gathered around the rail to get a better view.

Woodward scanned every inch of the horizon, looking for signs of a human, but could see nothing but choppy whitecaps. The tide was coming in.

As the gap between the cutter and the wreck closed, Woodward realized saving the vessel was a lost cause. Every inch of it was either on fire or had already sunk. Also, alongside it, the skeleton of another craft was in flames.

Suddenly, Woodward sighted something floating in the debris. He squinted, scrutinizing the wreckage.

Three heads bobbed in the water near some floating planks.

"Damn!" said Woodward. "There're three survivors out there. Take the wheel, will you, Bill, and notify the station. I'm going to tell the lieutenant to ready up the Avon."

"Roger," Watkins said. He keyed in the mike. "Channel Islands, this is the *Blackfin*. We have visual contact with three swimmers. We are maneuvering to effect a rescue. Stand by, Station."

"Roger, *Blackfin*. Channel Islands standing by. Over."

Woodward proceeded to the stern of the cutter and pulled the lieutenant aside.

The lieutenant began to issue commands for rescue by the Avon.

Woodward peered through the binoculars again. He saw a large triangular dorsal fin cutting through the water. "Oh shit!" he shouted. "There's a shark out there!"

Lieutenant Barnes yelled at a petty officer. "Barlow. Shark starboard of the survivors! Break out the M-16!"

"I see it!" Petty Officer Ed Barlow, a dark haired man in his early thirties, was the best shot on the boat. He ran to the stern, grabbed the M-16 and returned to the railing.

"Oh, Jesus, it's a great white!" the lieutenant shouted.

The dorsal fin cut steadily through the water toward the three swimmers.

"Go for a head shot!" the lieutenant yelled.

Barlow raised the gun.

Suddenly, the fin reared up out of the water, and Woodward saw the monstrous tail flash into the air.

Barlow fixed the M-16 on semiautomatic and squeezed the trigger. The first round fell short, kicking up a splash only inches behind the shark's wake.

Barlow's next round ripped through the head of the animal directly behind the eyes.

The tail immediately flew up in the water. The body jerked spasmodically for a moment as the monstrous animal floundered and then righted itself.

Barlow emptied another eight rounds directly at the head.

The shark twitched and almost leapt out of the water. Then its gigantic body slammed down onto the surface. It rolled over, displaying its white underbelly, and sank.

All that was left was a series of gigantic ripples and the acrid smell of cordite floating across the cutter's deck.

Cheers and applause arose from the crew.

Ecstatically, Woodward raised his arm in the air. "All right!"

The crew lowered the Avon into the water.

Johnny Bailey and Ed Connolly hopped into the craft. Bailey started the motor and they headed out to the swimmers.

The small craft moved in to the first swimmer. Blood was streaming from his body.

"Hey, that's Mike Gallagher, isn't it ?" Bailey asked.

Connolly nodded. "Sure is. Damn, it looks like the shark already had a bite."

Bailey reached out and grabbed the swimmer's good arm and lifted him out of the water.

Gasping for breath, Mike fell into the boat. He was bleeding badly and spitting up blood.

"He's gonna need medical assistance fast," Bailey said. Make him a tourniquet, will you? I'll get the other two swimmers on board."

Bailey took a piece of cloth from the medical kit while the small craft proceeded to the other two swimmers. Bailey was surprised to recognize one of them. "Hey, I know that guy — he's my dentist."

Connolly grinned. "Well, maybe he'll give you a discount on your next visit."

Bailey winked. "Let's hope so. His rates are sky-high."

The Avon approached the survivors.

"Johnny Bailey!" Buck shouted. "Boy, am I glad to see you!"

"You two okay?" Bailey asked.

"I'm okay," Buck said. "My wife's got a few cuts and bruises. But Mike Gallagher's pretty bad off. You'd better get him to a hospital ASAP."

Bailey reached out and grabbed Buck's hand while Connolly pulled Lynn, now fully conscious, onto the Avon.

Twilight settled in as they motored back to the cutter.

In only moments, the three were helped aboard the *Blackfin*.

Mike Gallagher was immediately taken to the berthing area on a stretcher. The crew brought towels and blankets for Buck and Lynn. Lynn followed Mike inside the covered cabin of the covered superstructure.

By the time Buck dried off, it was dark. Cathy had been in that cave for eight hours. Would she still be alive?

He wrapped the blanket around his shoulders as he was introduced to the rest of the crew from the Ventura County Sheriff's Department.

The Coast Guard team, consisting of another four crew members, finished setting out the dive equipment.

"What in the world happened out here?" A tall, middle-aged man with a square chin approached Buck. His piercing blue eyes stared quizzically.

"Who are you?" Buck asked.

"Sergeant Humphries. Ventura County Sheriff's Department. What's going on?"

"That guy you took inside is the captain of the boat, Mike Gallagher. He tried to kill his wife and me," Buck said. "He killed Pete. He left Cathy down in the cave to die. When I tried to save her, he tried to stop me with a gun. The fuel lines were broken when he fired the gun. When my wife started the engine, everything blew."

"Hold it, hold it," Humphries said, raising his hands. "You say he killed somebody?"

"Oh, yes," Buck nodded. "Pete Kendall."

"Hey, Sheriff," Simmons shouted from the rail of the boat. He had turned on his flashlight and was shining it in the water. "There's a body floating in the water!"

Humphries rushed to the rail. "Where is it?" he asked.

Buck joined the rest of the crew who were peering into the darkening waters.

Simmons shone his flashlight over Pete's mangled remains.

Humphries turned away from the scene. "Who the hell's that?" He shot a glance at Buck.

"That's Pete. He tried to help. He brought extra tanks. But Mike shot him dead and then the white got him."

Humphries shook his head. "Damn," he said. He raised his eyebrows. "You people are going to have to come down to the station for questioning." He paused. "What's going on with the girl below?"

"Cathy Gallagher? She's still in the cave," Buck said. "We need to get her out."

"Hey, Sheriff, I think I saw a shark fin out there," Simmons shouted. "A blue." His flashlight beam made a circle on the water.

"Hell, the blood is attracting sharks," Humphries said. "We've got to get that body out of the water, or we'll have every shark in the area around this boat. Get the Coast Guard to give us a hand, will you, Johnny?"

"Right." Johnny conferred with two of the crew.

One of the Coast Guard crew grabbed a gaff, hooked the body in the back and pulled it to the deck.

As Pete's body was lowered onto the cutter, it left a trail of blood in its wake.

Humphries turned to Buck. "What the hell were you doing out here?"

"Lobster hunting."

"Lobster hunting!" Humphries pursed his lips. "I've pulled nine corpses out of here over the past fifteen years. Don't you know this place is dangerous?"

Buck shrugged and gazed at the deck of the cutter.

Simmons joined them. "The divers are gearing up, Sergeant," he said. "But they're getting a little nervous about the safety factor. Someone's spotted a blue."

"Tell them to take the bang stick. The blues probably won't attack, but we'd better not take any chances."

"Yes sir." Simmons turned on his heels and headed for the divers.

Sergeant Humphries directed his gaze to Buck. "Do you know where the girl is located?"

"Sort of," Buck said.

"Well, then, we'd better get started," Humphries said.

"Can you give us a layout of this cave?"

Buck nodded in relief.

Finally, he could get back to his original mission — rescuing Cathy.

CHAPTER

20

A<small>LL THE DIVERS FROM</small> Search and Rescue gathered around
Buck as he explained the conditions of the impending
dive.

"Not only can I give you a layout," Buck responded
enthusiastically. "I can lead you in. But once we're in, I
don't know..." he hesitated. "That cave is really complex."

"You got out," Humphries began.

Buck nodded. "Yeah. Just barely."

"How far in do you think she is?"

Buck reflected for a moment. "Approximately 250
feet."

Humphries took out a pen and notepad from his pocket
and gave it to Buck. "Here, sketch us a picture. Johnny's
dived it, but the others are pretty much in the dark, so to
speak."

Buck began to draw a map of the cave. Odd, he
thought, the tunnels looked exactly like root canals. He

studied the diagram and then handed the map to Johnny. "This is the basic layout," he said, as the divers closed in for a look. "I left markers – an air tank, gloves and my orange bug bag."

"So, is that all we've got — markers?" Humphries asked.

Buck shook his head. "No. Cathy's got a flashlight. If she's flashing, we'll see the light."

"Great." Humphries grinned. "Okay, we've got fresh tanks and we're ready to go. Time is of the essence here. Buck and Johnny are going to be the primary divers. We'll need you two to lead us into the tunnel." He turned to Buck. "Let me give you a run-down of how my team operates."

He gave Connolly a slap on the back. "Connolly, here, is our line handler. He'll also have a bang stick with him just in case the big fish get a little feisty." Humphries pointed to the stick. It was three feet long, loaded with a shotgun shell at the end. "Hopefully, we won't have to use this," he said. "It works only by direct contact with the animal. He'll keep the stick cocked, but, let me warn you, it only has one shell. It has to be reloaded after each shot." He paused. "Connolly will go with you to the entrance of the tunnel, but that's all. Buck will attach his line to Connolly's. Any problems, you just tug on the line. He'll relay it to Daniels to get help. Got that?"

Buck nodded. "Got it."

Humphries pointed to Simmons. "Simmons is our safety diver. He floats at the entrance of the main chamber. He also carries a spare air tank. Once Buck and Johnny find the girl, Simmons will give Connolly the spare tank." He thumped Simmons on the shoulder.

Buck flashed him a thumbs-up.

Humphries turned to Daniels. "Now, Daniels is our

dive communication manager. He acts as a backup and also communicates anything from my line handler to my safety diver."

Buck nodded at Daniels, then Humphries.

"Okay," Humphries said, facing them all. "Then, we're ready to dive, boys."

"You done much night diving?" Johnny asked, grabbing his mask and fins.

Buck nodded. "Yeah. I'm not worried about the dark. I'm worried about the sharks." He slipped into his wet suit.

"You and me, both." Johnny wrapped his BC around his chest and turned to the team. "The surge is running strong. Let's follow the anchor line down. I'll tie my line to it."

Buck nodded.

The divers slipped into the rest of their gear. Buck led the way to the dive step, followed by Bailey, Simmons, Connolly and Daniels.

Buck took one last look at the sliver of a quarter moon in the sky, then stepped fins first off the dive step, plummeting into liquid darkness. He felt the impact of ripples as Johnny hit the water directly behind him.

Buck shone his flashlight around until he spotted the anchor line. He grabbed it and started down. As the divers descended the line like a ladder, the only illumination was the cone of his flashlight in the dark.

Buck descended quickly. The water was cold. To make matters worse, the surge was so bad, it had laid the kelp flat. Knowing how important it was to hang on, he clung to the line. Without the line, he could be swept away.

He remained focused and avoided shining the flashlight around him. Beginning divers often shone the flashlight in a circle, but that didn't accomplish anything except attract the sharks. Still, it was hard not to get the willies. Every now and then, he thought he sensed something large racing past, although he couldn't see a damned thing. He knew if he ran head on into a blue, it could attack.

With luck, the blues would be hovering around the other side of the boat where the body had been floating. He knew the flashlight might attract them, but he was at a loss without it.

Suddenly, Buck felt a tremendous force, pushing him sideways. He shone his flashlight in the direction of the impact. It reflected the luminescence of large round fish eyes directly in front of him.

Buck's blood froze. Oh, shit! It was a blue. The eyes headed straight toward him.

Instantly, he saw a blinding flash of teeth. He ducked down, his body just barely missing the onslaught of the animal. Goddamn! His heart pounded like crazy. The animal swooped past him and disappeared into the depths.

Instantly, all the divers followed the shark's pathway with their flashlights, hoping to sight the blue in case it tried for an ambush attack from below. But they saw nothing in the inky water except the ghostly stalks of kelp swaying with the surge.

Suddenly, Johnny tapped him on the shoulder.

Uh, oh! They had trouble. Directly above them, cruising the area, was another blue, perhaps ten feet in length.

Buck felt a powerful surge of water slamming against his back. He jerked his body around and saw glowing fish eyes from below, and then, coming directly for him — the gaping open jaws of the blue.

This time, Buck didn't have time to move. The animal raced directly toward him at a rapid-fire speed — twenty feet, ten, five. He felt his body cramping up in horror as he crouched, waiting for the teeth to clamp down on his flesh.

From out of the corner of his eye, he saw Connolly's bang stick swing by him and the tip make contact with the glowing right eye of the shark.

The fluorescent eye exploded into particles of blood and flesh, the charge passing directly through the head. Stunned, the great animal halted, just feet away from Buck. Blood streamed into the water.

Buck felt a flurry of water from above. He looked up to see the other blue now swimming over them. Abruptly, it circled and then moved in for attack. Before he could dart away, it was coming for him. Oh, Jesus! He'd never make it!

Connolly fumbled with the shell, trying to reload the bang stick, while the blue rushed toward him with light-ning speed. It was impossible for Connolly to reload the stick in time.

The shark propelled its body forward like a torpedo, its great mouth open, ready to gash flesh. Buck felt a monstrous rush of water and then right before his eyes, the long pointed snout dove toward him, jaws open wide.

But the shark whizzed past Buck, the scythe-like tail slapping him in the face. The blue snatched the smaller shark in its mouth and snapped it in half.

A wave of relief washed over Buck. He closed his eyes. He opened them to see the blue's teeth ripping through the other shark's carcass.

Half of the carcass floated downwards into the black abyss while the rest was devoured. Waves rippled past the divers, as the blue flung the carcass from side to side in its jaws.

Buck watched the cannibalistic scene in horror. But the others were already hand signaling for him to move,

urging him forward. Once the blue had finished its feeding frenzy, it would be ready for another attack. In minutes, they would be in danger again. There was no time
to waste.

He clung to the line where it changed to chain and
finally, hit bottom. He quickly located the line Mike had
tied to the rock. As they got closer, it took all his strength
not to be slammed into the cave rock by the surge, because the cave acted like a suction cup, funneling the
water into it.

Inside the entrance to the chamber, the divers went to
work. Daniels began attaching a line from his weight belt
to Connolly's and finally, to Buck. The line would unreel
from Buck's waist. All Buck had to do was tug on the line
for help.

Buck started toward the back of the cave, using the
line he had tied earlier for direction.

Johnny and Connolly followed.

Once they hit the back of the cave, Buck searched the
jagged rocks until he found the entrance to the tunnel. He
signaled to the two divers.

Connolly settled down at the entrance. Buck started
out into the tunnel with Johnny following him, using the
line from Buck's belt to get his direction.

Buck shone his flashlight back. Luckily, the silt had
dissipated. He could see more clearly now. He started
back into the tunnel with Johnny immediately behind him.
There were crevices and pockets everywhere.

After going back some, he found the glove he had
dropped at the turn of the tunnel. In five more minutes, he
found Cathy's cylinder. He went back farther, but all the
crevices looked the same.

He was becoming disoriented. He went to the bottom,
trying to find the second glove he had used for a marker,

but, he couldn't find it. He must have covered it up in his fight with Mike in the cave.

Buck had a sinking feeling in the pit of his stomach. They could search for days in this tunnel and never find Cathy.

He turned around and shook his head, shrugging at Johnny.

Johnny waved his hands, indicating they had to take a different approach. He tapped Buck on the shoulder and pointed toward the exhaust bubbles from the regulators.

That was an idea! If they could find out where the air bubbles were congregating, they could locate the pockets in the cave. Instead of looking for his markers, Buck began watching the pattern of the bubbles.

He floated up, exploring one of the cracks where the bubbles were going. Sure enough, in the distance, was a mirrorlike surface that might represent air. His heart starting beating excitedly. This just might be the right chamber.

He swam closer, broke the surface of the water and immediately shone the flashlight beam upward.

The light stopped only a few feet away. This air pocket wasn't large enough to be the cavern he and Cathy had found. His heart sank. Shaking his head, he ducked back in the water and swam down to Johnny.

Was this going to work, he wondered? All these tunnels looked the same.

Still, the pattern of the air bubbles was their only hope. The two finned upward again.

Buck squinted. Was that a flashlight beam? Or only an illusion? He motioned to Johnny and swam toward the light. This must be the place. The crevice was large enough for two bodies to enter.

He plunged into the mercury-like bubble and when he hit the surface, he immediately took his regulator out of his mouth. "Cathy," he shouted. "Cathy Gallagher, are you in here?"

The flashlight beam bounced off the walls.

He saw Cathy huddled in the corner of the cave. But she didn't answer him and she wasn't moving. The flashlight lay beside her in the cave, its light dimming with each passing second. Had she just passed out? Or was she dead?

CHAPTER

21

"CATHY, CATHY!"

Cathy Gallagher heard a voice calling her name. But she was far, far away from the voice, drifting away, down a long, long tunnel towards another destination. She was rowing in a small wooden boat toward someone far off in the distance.

She ignored the voice. Just up ahead was a figure clothed in black. She could not recognize it. Yet, it was so familiar. It was waving to her, signaling to her. Just there, just on the other side. She was getting closer and closer, no longer distant.

The figure reached out for her. She could not see his face, although she knew him immediately. It was Mike. And who was that beside him? Was it Jonathan? Yes, the small black figure was Jonathan.

"Mama!" he cried.

In a short while, they would all be together. Mike would take her hand and there would be a finality to their reunion. They would never be apart again.

She saw Mike distinctly now, a strand of blond hair hanging over his face, his glowing smile growing more and more recognizable. "Take my hand, Cathy," he said. "Just take my hand. I'll hold onto you forever."

She stopped rowing, put down the oars and reached out for his hand.

His arms extended, ghostly and slow.

She felt safe with him. In a moment, she would be his. She felt just the tip of his fingers touch her palm.

"Will you take my hand, Cathy?" he asked.

"Yes, Mike," she said. "Yes!"

"Cathy!" the voice shouted.

She gasped. There was something pressing against her mouth, crushing down on her, pushing against her nostrils. She gasped, coughed, tried to push it away. She fought it off.

He was disappearing! Mike was leaving her! And Jonathan. Jonathan was going!

"No!" she shouted. "No!"

She tried to grasp them, but they were gone. Her fingertips felt only air.

The regulator was pushing down on her mouth, forcing her to breathe. A sound of wind beat around her ears. She felt herself being pulled back by strong arms, rushing through a tunnel of darkness, thrown onto a barren shore, crashing against jagged rocks. She coughed, sputtered, breathed in the air, and then there was a great wrenching in her stomach.

"Look out, she's gonna throw up!" a voice shouted.

She retched and gagged. The regulator was pulled out of her mouth as she vomited into the water below. She vomited again and reached for the regulator. It was thrust once more against her face.

She took a deep breath. She couldn't seem to get

enough air.

"You okay, Cathy?" a male voice asked.

She turned to the light, took the regulator out of her mouth for a moment. "Mike?" she gasped. "Mike."

"No, it's Buck, Cathy. Buck."

"Buck," she said. "Buck." She looked into his face.

He had taken his regulator out of his mouth to talk. It was Buck with his sandy hair and his wide grin staring at her. He was propped up on the ledge beside her. She saw another figure in the water.

"This is Johnny," Buck said. "He's with a rescue team, Cathy. We've come to get you out of here."

She coughed and took note of her surroundings. Where was she? She remembered — she was in a cave on Santa Cruz Island. Mike had let go of her hand and she'd gotten lost. Buck had left to get help.

"Buck, I thought you were dead."

"I'm as alive as you are, Cathy," Buck said.

"Where's Mike?"

Buck paused. He turned away from her for a moment, took a breath from his regulator and spoke. "He's topside, Cathy."

She sighed in relief. Mike was okay. "Mike and I are never going to be apart again."

Buck nodded. "Sure, Cathy." He looked away from her for a moment. "Meanwhile, we've got to get you out of here. Do you think you can make it out?"

"Yeah," she gasped.

"We've got a rescue team in the main chamber. I want you to breathe from my regulator while I help you into your BC, okay?"

She nodded. She put her hand to her pounding head. Everything was reeling around her. She put the regulator in her mouth and took a deep breath.

"I know you don't feel well, but you've got to concentrate on making it out of here, Cathy. You'll need to hold onto the line, even though you're still pretty weak. You follow Johnny. I'll be right behind you. Once we get out of the cave, it will be dangerous getting up. It's night. The sharks are out and the surge is running strong. As long as you hold onto the line, you'll be okay. Do you think you can do it?"

"Yeah, I can do it, Buck," she said.

Buck propped himself up on the ledge. He grabbed another bottle from Johnny and hoisted it up on the ledge. He helped Cathy into her gear.

"Well, let's get going, Cathy," Johnny grinned at her. "We don't want to keep the rest of the guys in suspense for too long."

The three of them slid down in the water. Johnny led with the flashlight, while Cathy followed and Buck brought up the rear.

Johnny guided them into the main chamber.

Cathy was struck by how easy it was moving through the silt with the line. All they needed was a pathway out.

They hit the main chamber quickly. She caught a glimpse of two other divers and another one at the entrance to the cave. The others joined them and they all started along the line to the entranceway.

As soon as they started out, a tremendous force pushed against her. Good God! The surge was fierce.

She held on with all her might to the line. But she wasn't expecting what happened next.

Near the entrance, she felt a surge slam against her body. She felt like she was battling a hurricane. She could barely hold onto the line.

Then, without warning, a huge swell caught her, lifted her up and jerked the line from her hand.

Buck immediately gripped her shoulder, but the swell ripped her body from his grasp.

She kicked hard, fighting back, but her legs were useless, like a rag doll's. She was thrown back into the chamber, out of sight of the other divers. Her dive light was ripped from her grasp to dangle useless from its lanyard around her wrist.

Finally, there was a lull in the swell and she managed to turn on the light. Just ahead was a rock. She grappled it and grabbed the dive light with the other hand, trying to relocate the line with her light.

She located the line and started out again, toward the other divers. But she'd gone only several feet when the next swell hit her even harder and she was torn again from the line.

The underwater light in her hand was snagged in a fissure in the rock. Her dive gloves were ripped from her hands. There was nothing she could do but grab a huge boulder, trying to hold onto that and hunker down against the impending surge.

She saw Buck coming back down the line. He held out his hand for her to grasp.

But another swell hit and immediately, she was crunched onto the rocks of the floor.

Her regulator was knocked from her mouth. Hurriedly, she found the hose and got the mouthpiece back. She had no idea where Buck was, or her own location.

The surge eventually pushed her into an alcove where she was able to get some protection.

Finally, she felt a strong hand reach out to her. It was Buck. He had managed to grab her again and was pulling her in.

The two of them waited for another lull, then clung to the line as they swam out of the cave. This time, they were able to miss the power of the surge.

Even though the surge was bad outside the chamber, the line made swimming possible. They climbed up the line as if scaling a wall, following the beam of Johnny's flashlight to the surface.

With the light shining upward, she could see the outline of the steel hull of the boat, swaying back and forth with the waves.

They all hit the surface about the same time. They rose into the predictable world of sea spray blowing against their masks.

Cathy turned around and saw the calm reassurance of the bow wobbling against the light, dipping into the chops against the pull of the anchor.

She pulled off her mask and looked up. Across the dark heavens, the sky was rich with stars, the brightest she'd ever seen.

CHAPTER

22

CATHY SWAM TOWARD THE stern of the cutter where the Coast Guard was waiting for the divers. As she put her foot on the dive step, strong arms helped her onto the lighted deck.

"Welcome to the *Blackfin*, ma'am," said one of the officers, as he helped her aboard. He smiled. "We're sure glad to see you."

"Not as glad as I am to see you." Cathy sat on the dive step as he pulled off her flippers and began to unsnap her BC.

"We'll get you warmed up and check your vitals. You could be hypothermic," he said, as he lifted off her tank and helped her out of her gear.

Cathy waved her hand. "I'm fine, really."

While the other officers helped Buck and the sheriff's department divers onto the boat, one of them hurried below and returned with heavy wool blankets and towels.

Cathy pulled off her wet suit as one of the officers wrapped a blanket over her bathing suit and around her shoulders.

The officer led her to a chair where a medic began to check her pulse and blood pressure.

She shivered. The night air was chilly. Large cups of steaming coffee were being passed around.

"All right," said the medic. "It looks like everything here is okay."

"I'd like one of those," she said, pointing to the coffee. "I haven't had anything to eat or drink for hours."

An officer brought her some coffee.

"Don't drink too fast," said the medic. "You'll throw up." He paused. "I've got to go back inside, ma'am. We've got someone else who needs emergency medical assistance."

She nodded, sipping the coffee slowly and letting the warm liquid dribble down her throat.

Exhausted, she sank back in a chair on the deck. She studied the crowd of men at the stern. Mike wasn't among them.

"Where's Mike?" she asked, turning to Buck.

Before he could answer, a tall middle-aged man approached her. "You okay, ma'am?" he asked.

She nodded. "Who are you?"

"Sergeant Humphries. Ventura County Sheriff's Department, Search and Rescue."

"I want to see my husband. Where is he?"

"Your husband's inside," Humphries nodded at the cabin. "I'd better warn you, he's hurt pretty bad."

"Hurt? What happened?"

"You didn't tell her?" Humphries asked, directing his gaze to Buck.

Buck shook his head.

Cathy felt dizzy. She put her hands to her head. "What's going on, Buck?"

Buck paused and took a deep breath. "Mike was attacked by a shark. He's lost an arm and his chest is torn open. He's lost a lot of blood. They've got him under sedation and the medic's giving him intravenous fluid."

Cathy felt her heart leap in her throat. "Is he gonna be okay?"

Humphries gave her a direct look. "We've called in a rescue helicopter from the mainland."

"Oh, God!" She jumped up. "I've got to see him."

Buck grabbed her arm. "Before you go in there, there's something I need to tell you, Cathy."

"What's that?"

Buck pursed his lips together in determination. "You were right about Mike."

"Right?" She frowned.

"Remember when you were down in that cave and you told me Mike purposefully let go of your hand."

"Yes," she said, slowly.

"Well, he did."

She felt a jolt of electricity race through her body. "He wanted to kill me?"

Buck nodded. "I didn't want to tell you down there. You might have panicked, done anything."

She opened her mouth in amazement. She'd suspected it all along. Still, she hadn't wanted to believe it was true.

God, what a bastard! He'd tried to kill her. He'd left her in that cave to die. "He tried to kill me...us?"

Buck nodded.

She put her head in her hands. She couldn't believe it.

"I was fighting him off when the shark attacked him," Buck said.

She opened her mouth in amazement. "That's why he didn't want you along on the trip. God, I'm so sorry for all this. I shouldn't have asked you."

Buck shook his head. "I'm just glad I did come along, Cathy. I'm afraid you'd be dead right now, if I didn't."

She shuddered. How could he do it? Who was Mike? She'd lived with this man, slept with him, shared memories with him, and now, she realized she'd never known him. He was a stranger. A killer.

She squared her shoulders and took a deep breath. "I've got to see him, Buck. Let go of my arm."

Buck shook his head. "Wait, Cathy, there's more...." he began.

"More?" she asked.

"Lynn's in there with him."

"Lynn...what is she doing in there?"

Buck paused. He looked at the deck of the cutter.

Cathy thought for a moment. She remembered the looks Mike gave Lynn when they were socializing at parties. She remembered how her husband was just a little too friendly with Lynn. She remembered the times they had shared her hot tub laughing quietly together while she and Buck went up to get drinks.

"They were having an affair," she said bluntly.

Buck nodded. "More than that. He planned to marry her."

Cathy put her hand to her mouth in amazement. She felt tears well up in her eyes. Her cheeks grew wet. She tried to wipe away the tears.

Buck pulled her to him and held her against his shoulder. "Go ahead and cry, Cathy," he said. "But, cry for yourself. Don't cry for that bastard of a husband. He's a cold-blooded murderer. He planned this thing from the start. He never expected you to get out of that cave."

Cathy felt overwhelmed. She fell into Buck's arms and sobbed.

After a few minutes, she pulled away from Buck. "I've

got to go in there," she said with determination. "I've got to see him."

"Are you sure?"

"Yes, I'm sure."

She turned away from Buck, strode toward the cabin and walked inside.

In the back, Mike lay on a cot. He was missing an arm. His right shoulder and chest were heavily bandaged.

On one side of the cot was the medic giving Mike an IV. On the other side was Lynn.

Sheriff Humphries followed her, but kept his distance, standing at the entrance as Cathy stared at the scene in front of her.

"We almost had it all, honey," Mike mumbled.

Lynn brushed back a strand of hair from his face. Tears were streaming down her cheeks. "Don't talk, Mike. The helicopter will be here soon."

"I would have married you, Lynn. You know that, don't you."

"I know, I know." She wiped the tears from her eyes. "Don't lose consciousness."

"Are you crying, Lynn?" he asked, reaching up to feel her face with his only remaining hand.

"Yes."

"Why?"

"I don't want you to die, Mike."

He coughed. "Ah, Lynn. I can't die. Navy SEALs never say die." He stared straight ahead. "Lynn, I can't see you. Where are you?"

"I'm right here, Mike," she said, leaning closer. "Just hold on. The helicopter will be here shortly."

The medic stood up and leaned over Mike. "You need to stay conscious," he said. "Talk to me, man." He began packaging him for the lift.

Overhead, Cathy heard the whirring of rotors from a helicopter growing louder by the second.

Mike grimaced. "Is that the helos I hear, Ed? Damn, this jungle's so dark, I can't see a thing. We've got to get out of here, man. We're under heavy fire."

"Talk to me, sir" the medic repeated. "What's your name?"

Mike coughed. "Shark Man of 'Nam," he said. Then he closed his eyes.

The medic leaned over, took his hand and felt his pulse. He looked at Lynn in alarm. He shook his head. "I'm afraid there's nothing more anyone can do." He began to detach the IV.

Lynn sat down in the chair, put her head in her hands and sobbed.

Cathy heard the sound of men jumping from the helicopter on the deck as it hovered above the cutter. Two men approached the door.

Cathy and Buck made way for the paramedics as they burst inside.

Walking outside, Cathy shook her head in confusion. "You were right, Buck. I shouldn't have gone in there."

Buck patted her gently on the shoulder.

Sheriff Humphries approached them. "That was your wife?" he asked, looking at Buck.

Buck nodded. "Yeah. She was having an affair with Mike. She planned to divorce me and marry him once Cathy was out of the way."

"That makes her a conspirator in attempted murder," the sheriff said. "I'm going to put in a call to homicide. They'll need to have a heads-up on what's been going on out here."

Buck nodded.

As the hook from the helicopter was lowered, one of

the crewmen grabbed a pole and touched the helicopter's hoist cable.

Cathy glanced back as the paramedics put Mike's body in a basket stretcher. The basket was hooked to the cable, the pole removed and the basket hoisted into the helicopter. Then the bird rose into the air and the whirring grew fainter and fainter.

Cathy shook her head. "Mike trying to kill me and then being attacked by a shark. I don't know whether to cry or curse him," she said.

She pulled the blanket tightly around her. She felt like her body was shutting down. She walked outside and slumped down in the deck chair again.

"Are you okay?" the sheriff asked, following her. "Do you want me to call the medic?"

"I don't need a medic," Cathy said. "I just need to be left alone for awhile."

Sheriff Humphries nodded. He turned away from her and walked back to the cabin.

Buck sat down beside her. He put his arm on her shoulder.

"I should have known, Buck," she said. "I knew he was having affairs. I just didn't know he was having one with my friend. What a fool I've been!"

He leaned back in the seat. "You could say that about me."

"How could I have been married to a man like that all those years?"

Buck shook his head. "Money does strange things to people."

She gritted her teeth. "I suppose so. Only I didn't think Mike was ever in the marriage just for the money!" She shook her head in disbelief. "Boy, was I wrong!"

Buck stared at the deck. "We were both wrong."

"Jeez, the truth hurts!"

"Yeah, it hurts me, too, Cathy."

The engines of the *Blackfin* revved up and a heavy smell of diesel exhaust hung in the air.

Cathy felt her stomach turn over. "I think I'm gonna be sick." She ran to the rail and vomited into the churning black water below.

She wiped her hand across her mouth and tried to regain her composure. Then she returned to the chair beside Buck.

The cutter pulled out of the cove and made its way into open water. Like a great black shadow, the island of Santa Cruz disappeared on the horizon.

The cutter raced through the water, waves slapping the hull.

Cathy raised her head and looked up to the heavens. A sliver of moon cut the blackness of the sky. Stars twinkled like a thousand diamonds.

She looked down at her hands and twisted the diamond engagement ring off her finger. Then, she took off her wedding ring and hurled them both into the ocean.

So long, Mike Gallagher. Good riddance.

The door opened and Sheriff Humphries approached them again. "We'll be at the Santa Barbara Harbor in about an hour and a half."

"Good," Cathy said. "I'm looking forward to being on dry land again."

She glanced back at the dive crew. They were milling around together at the back of the cutter, whispering and staring at her. One of them pointed.

"Why are they whispering like that?" Cathy asked. "You'd think they'd seen a ghost."

"Well, ma'am," Humphries winked. "To them, you are a ghost. You're the first live one they've brought up from these caves."

Cathy smiled and waved at the crew. "I'm alive!" she shouted.

They clapped and cheered.

Ghosts.

Well, maybe she was a ghost. Maybe she was one of those Edgar Allan Poe heroines come back from the nether world. Risen from the dead. "I guess I am a ghost in a way," she said, solemnly glancing at Buck. "I feel like I died down there. I know my past life is over."

Buck glanced up at the stars. "Yes, Cathy. I believe you're right."

"How are we going to live again, Buck?"

Buck pursed his lips. "Give it some time, Cathy. Just give it some time."

CHAPTER

23

BUCK SAT AT HIS favorite table at Brophy's. He had just finished lunch with a colleague.

He had a panoramic view of the marina. It was a glorious November day. Bright midday sunlight glinted off the sailboat masts. The sea was calm. Not a wave in sight. He noticed the *Blackfin* was docked right below him.

On the far horizon, the island of Santa Cruz rose in the mist as if it were floating, detached from ocean and sky.

Santa Cruz. The name meant Holy Cross in Spanish. He'd heard it had been named after an expedition of Spanish friars who had left behind a walking stick with a small iron cross on its handle.

The waitress interrupted his thoughts. "Here's your check, sir."

He paid his bill and walked to his car, parked in the lot not far from the restaurant.

He drove down State Street to the historic district and

parked in the lot behind his office. He got out of the car and made his way to the front of the white stucco building.

He passed a priest dressed in black pants and shirt with a white collar. The priest was walking toward Our Lady of Sorrows Church.

Buck nodded politely to the priest. He hadn't noticed it before, but Santa Barbara was a city of churches. There seemed to be a parish or church or monastery on every other corner.

He passed through the courtyard of the building with its twisted vines of magenta bougainvillea shading the courtyard, then up the stairs to his second story office with "CHRISTOPHER B. CONNORS, DMD" printed on the door.

He waved at the receptionist as he walked past her.

"Mrs. Gallagher is already here," his receptionist said.

"Tell her I'll be with her in just a moment." He went to a back room and changed into his scrubs.

Buck walked down the hallway to the room where the nurse had put Cathy Gallagher, picked up her chart and scanned it quickly.

When he entered the room, he found his assistant had already put the radiographs on the view box. Although the images appeared normal, the vitality tests were a little off. He would be performing a root canal on number fifteen this morning.

"Cathy," he said, smiling. "How are you?"

"Well, my tooth is killing me. But other than that, I'm doing fine. How are you holding up?"

"I'm managing."

Buck reflected. The sensationalism had certainly given him plenty of notoriety. There'd been a trial. His wife had been convicted as a conspirator in attempted murder.

He'd received a lot of publicity, not all of it good.

Some of his dentist friends who preferred status to good dentistry didn't like referring patients to a doctor whose wife was a jailbird. But others didn't seem to mind.

After all the events unfolded, he seemed to have become a hero to most. Thank God his name was exonerated, because it was a household word in Santa Barbara.

"I'd definitely say publicity is not a problem for me, Cathy," he added.

He'd had his picture in the paper for weeks. At the height of the publicity, several film companies had jumped on the story for a TV Movie-of-the-Week. It had all the right ingredients — murder, underwater adventure, sharks, a nearly fatal rescue and scandal surrounding a former movie star.

But, he'd firmly declined all offers. He just couldn't bring himself to talk about the incident. It was too personal. Maybe, in time....

Time was supposed to heal all wounds. At least that was what they said. But he would never forget.

Even twenty years from now, he knew that November day on Santa Cruz Island would be vivid in his mind. Incidents like that were like snapshots in your life. They stood out while other images faded.

He could still remember as if it were yesterday — that frightened look in Cathy's eyes when he left her in the cave, perhaps forever; the gut-wrenching sight of silent agony on Mike's face when the white yanked his arm from his body; that angry backwards glance from Lynn when the sheriff led her in handcuffs to the squad car.

"Hey, you look like you are miles away," Cathy commented.

Buck looked up. "Yeah. I guess I was. Just thinking

about Santa Cruz."

"It's been almost a year since that day, Buck. We should be grateful we're both here, today."

He smiled. "I'm grateful we're alive, Cathy. It's a miracle."

She nodded.

"You know, Cathy, I went back to Santa Cruz, just to see that cave. The water was crystal clear. I dove down and saw that opening where we went. Light was streaming through the tunnel opening and I could see clearly inside it. It sure seems weird that we almost lost our lives in there. Conditions can really change on those islands."

"That goes for life too, huh, Buck?"

"Yeah," agreed Buck, reflecting.

Cathy changed the subject. "How are the kids?"

"Okay. Of course, they know their mother's in jail, but I haven't told them the whole story. Maybe when they're older..."

"I know it's been rough on them in school."

He nodded. "Yeah, it has. But we're coping. We finally moved into a smaller house last week. We've got a lot of unpacking to do, but we're doing just fine."

Buck thought for a moment. He was having to do with a lot less these days. Yet he really didn't need the high-priced home and cars. He had his kids and his friends and that was what was important in life.

He had striven so hard in the past for prestige and money, just to keep Lynn happy and his family together. All he had wanted had been love from his kids and his wife. But, money had torn them apart. It had destroyed the Gallaghers' marriage and his.

Cathy interrupted his thoughts. "I hear you have a new girlfriend, Buck."

"Yeah." Buck beamed. "Actually, she's one of the

teachers in the school. She really took an interest in Scotty when his grades started falling off during the trial. I was all wound up, not there for him as much as I could be, and with his mother in jail, well...he just didn't have anyone around except for Sally Hawkins. I was glad she was there for him...and later for me." Sally was certainly different from Lynn.

"How about you, Cathy?" Buck asked. "How are you doing?"

"Well, I finally sold the dive business." She paused. "I've actually started taking some underwater photographs again. I may get back into it, open up another shop. I guess I just set aside my own needs when I was married to Mike."

Buck nodded. "I know somebody you might like to meet. A real nice guy. He's a friend of mine, a surgeon."

"Well, maybe later, Buck. I don't think I'm ready for a man in my life quite yet."

"Well, all men aren't like Mike. And all women aren't like Lynn."

"Buck, let me ask you something," she said. "I've felt a little different ever since the incident. I mean, I thought maybe I found God in that cave. Did you see God?"

He smiled, reflecting for a moment. "A lot of people have asked me that question, Cathy. Let's just say I made my peace with God."

"Oh." Cathy wrinkled her brow.

"Well, I guess we'd better stop all this chatting and start doing this root canal. "

"Go ahead."

He hesitated. "You know I don't like to do anything unless I'm sure that tooth is necrotic. I'd like some more scientific evidence."

"You dentists are worse than priests." She laughed.

"The big question used to be 'Can this marriage be saved?' Now it's 'Can this tooth be saved?' I have never had so much trouble getting a root canal. That's a bad tooth, Buck."

"There's no evidence," he argued. "All the instruments, the machines say..." he began.

A spark of anger raced through her eyes. "The evidence is inside. It's me." Cathy pointed to herself. "I know. I'm in pain. I feel it."

"But how do you know it's that tooth?" he began.

"I just know. Sometimes all you've to go on is just faith, Buck. You gotta listen to yourself — trust your own feelings." She paused.

He sighed. "All right, Cathy. Here goes."

Buck put on his gloves. He examined the radiograph. "Looks like you've got a difficult root, Cathy. This may take a little while."

"Well, then the sooner we get started, the better."

He nodded. Supposedly, the bad tooth was number fifteen — the upper left, second molar. She'd been blaming a lot of headaches on it.

He gave her a local infiltration of xylocaine to anesthetize the posterior superior alveolar nerve. After he got into the tooth, he found one canal was necrotic.

He looked at the radiographs. He was a scientist, but in this case the radiographs were wrong. They showed nothing. So much for scientific evidence, he thought, shaking his head, perplexed.

Cathy shifted in her seat. It was probably just the sound of the drill that made her flinch. Still, he stopped.

"You okay?" he asked.

She nodded.

He patted her kindly on the shoulder. "I promise you, you won't feel a thing."

She nodded again.

His assistant smiled at both of them.

He took one of his number 06 files, and began to work his way down into the canal. One of the roots had a long curved end. Luckily, he had a pathfinder that could negotiate tight corners.

Making his way down the canal, he passed a calcium deposit. He didn't know if the canal might lead to another and branch off in a different direction or if it was just one canal. The radiographs didn't show everything. He gently removed more of the debris.

As he worked, his mind returned to Santa Cruz Island. He remembered the words of the old priest in the boarding school. He remembered swimming away from Cathy and the vision he'd had in the cave. It had reminded him of a giant root canal.

How had he known that tunnel was the right one? He hadn't had any outside evidence to back him up. All he'd had was a feeling — just faith.

Slowly, an idea began to take shape.

Life was sort of like a root canal, he thought, with strange twists and passageways. When least expected, it could take a turn, lead you up a blind alley or down another.

His ideas about life had changed since that day in the cave. He'd always thought science was enough to get through life. But life was too complicated. It wasn't scientific. It wasn't black and white like a radiograph. It didn't follow straight lines.

Just when you thought things were going along fine, life would throw you a curve and turn your life upside down.

Science wasn't enough. There were too many unexpected surprises, too many tragedies, too much sorrow.

He had lost his wife. He had lost his home. He had almost lost his life. He had to start all over again.

So much tragedy. So many losses. How could you deal with all those losses? How could you deal with unexpected surprises?

What had kept him from panicking down in that cave? What had gotten him through to the light at the end of the tunnel? Just faith.

Life was like a root canal, or better yet, it was more...like a labyrinth.

Sometimes, the obstacles seemed insurmountable; everything around you was black. You were dead in the water.

But, in life, all you could do was have faith, plunge into it and hope for the best. You either sank or you swam.

If you were lucky, like he had been, then it all worked out in the end. You swam. You met the challenges, overcame the hurdles and moved on.

You had to be lucky, he thought, but you needed more than luck to make it through life.

"There, that ought to do it, Cathy," he said, as he put the sealer in her tooth. "This tooth was definitely the source of the problem. You'll be like new again in no time."

She nodded.

The operation would be over in a moment. He'd gotten rid of the necrotic pulp that was giving her the problem. He'd prescribe a little pain killer for her and send her on her way. In no time, she'd be feeling herself again.

Cathy responded with a muffled "thank you." She couldn't do much more with the xylocaine in her jaw.

Yes, he thought, you had to have more than luck when you went through life. You had to have a little faith. And, even then, you just couldn't go on blind faith.

What had Lynn called him? A canal master? Yes, you

had to be able to negotiate the twists and turns, the unexpected surprises and the dead ends. You had to be a
canal master, as well.